Sibley, Celestine.

A plague of kinfolks.

$20.00

DATE			

A Plague of Kinfolks

ALSO BY CELESTINE SIBLEY

Dire Happenings at Scratch Ankle

Straight as an Arrow

Ah, Sweet Mystery

Christmas in Georgia

Dear Store

A Place Called Sweet Apple

Especially at Christmas

Mothers Are Always Special

Sweet Apple Gardening Book

Day by Day

Small Blessings

Jincey

Children, My Children

Young'uns

The Magical Realm of Sallie Middleton (co-author)

Turned Funny

Tokens of Myself

Peachtree Street U.S.A.: An Affectionate Portrait of Atlanta

For All Seasons

The Malignant Heart

A Plague of Kinfolks

A Kate Mulcay Mystery

CELESTINE SIBLEY

HarperCollins*Publishers*

HarperCollins books may be purchased for educational, business, or sales promotional use. For information please write: Special Markets Department, HarperCollins Publishers, Inc., 10 East 53rd Street, New York, NY 10022.

FIRST EDITION

Designed by Caitlin Daniels

Sibley, Celestine.
A plague of kinfolks : a Kate Mulcay mystery / Celestine Sibley. — 1st ed.
p. cm.
ISBN 0-06-017704-7
1. Mulcay, Kate (Fictitious character)—Fiction. I. Title.
PS35369.I256P58 1995 94-39142
813'.54—dc20

---

95 96 97 98 99 ❖/HC 10 9 8 7 6 5 4 3 2 1

For my grandchildren, John, Bird, Sibley, Ted, Susy, David, John Steven, and Betsy, and my great-grandchildren, Vincent and Wolfie.

Kate Mulcay had no relatives that she knew of, and as far as she knew her late husband, Police Lieutenant Benjamin Mulcay, had only some remote cousins out West somewhere.

So she was caught unawares when the telephone pulled her in from the backyard that summer afternoon and a man's voice said exuberantly, "Cousin Kate! How in the world are you? Guess who this is!"

If there was anything Kate hated more than having her struggles to prune the New Dawn rose interrupted, it was the guess-who-this-is game. As a newspaper columnist she was often invited by old-time Atlantans to guess who had moved back to town after a sojourn in Des Moines or Schenectady. This time, with thorns from the New Dawn digging into her wrists and forearms and dripping droplets of blood on the kitchen phone, she stubbornly refused to guess.

"I don't know," she said. "Suppose you tell me."

"Aw, come on, Cuz, be a sport," the voice entreated.

"Does the name 'Little Edge' or 'Edgie' mean anything to you?"

Kate wanted to snap, *Not a thing . . . good-bye!* But she was a lifelong listener to telephone solicitors and street-corner tract distributors. She even invited in and served coffee to door-to-door salesmen. It was risky, friends told her; but not to listen to people, even jerks, could be risky, too. That "jerk" could be you, she thought.

She wiped the blood off her arm onto her blue jeans and said patiently, "I'm not sure. Possibly. Are you related to my husband, Benjy? I can't seem to remember."

"A touch of the old Alzheimer's!" he cried gaily. "Well, I reckon we're all getting old enough. As a matter of fact, Ben and I are—were—cousins. Once or twice removed . . . I don't keep up with that. But his mother's relatives settled in Beeville, Texas, and that's where I come in. Aunt Buena's grandson."

"Oh," said Kate faintly. She was beginning to remember—something. Long before she and Benjy were married or even before they knew they could stand one another, he flew jets in the Marines and was once stationed somewhere in Texas. He said he had spent a weekend with some of his mother's people.

Well, she thought wanly, Benjy's chickens have come home to roost . . . on me.

"You're Edge?" she asked.

"That's right. Edgeworth Green, called Edgie or Little Edge. My daddy was Big Edge. I sure am looking forward to meeting you. I heard Ben had himself a looker and when I decided to come to Atlanta, nothing would do but I look you up." He paused and then mumbled awkwardly, "I was sorry to hear about Ben's death."

That single sentence softened Kate. "You are in Atlanta?" she said. "Well, why don't you come on out to see me? I live in a log cabin north of Roswell and this is my day off, so I'll be free."

"Super," said Little Edge. "I stopped at the newspaper office to see if you were there and got your number. I can probably get directions from somebody. Oh, yeah, my wife Bambi is with me and she'll be tickled to death to meet you."

Kate hung up the phone. The "looker," she thought dispiritedly, examining her reflection in the little mirror over the kitchen phone and pushing her straight, gray-flecked brown hair back from her sweaty brow. She hadn't been considered a "looker" back when she was the age for it, and now, past middle age, her once good-humored, freckled face looked like a bundle of sticks—lines between the eyes, lines around the eyes, pleats on the upper lip. Even Benjy, who loved her and looked after her, had never called her pretty. He did like what he called her tattletale brown eyes, which allegedly revealed every thought, feeling, or impulse she had. Or so he had said. Kate hoped not.

Since Benjy died, Kate hadn't thought much about her appearance. She washed her hair in the shower with whatever soap was handy, got it cut when it began to drift into her eyes and drag on the collars of her blouses. She bought cream meant for dry skin and forgot to use it. If she couldn't find a lipstick in her rush to get out the door and to the MARTA bus or train in the morning, it didn't bother her.

Now she wished vaguely that she looked better, if Benjy's distant kin had closed the distance and were coming to see her. She knew Benjy had never called her a "looker," but he had probably said something to Aunt Buena, whoever she was, to indicate that he thought well of the girl he had married.

Kate sighed. The best she could do was divest herself of her grubby jeans and sneakers, take a shower, and put on a dress. She'd just have to postpone pruning the New Dawn rose and training it over the arbor by the back porch. It was to have been her main achievement for her Saturday off. The pale pink roses had filled the air with sweetness only a month or two earlier and Kate had read that they might do a repeat performance in late summer. They never had before, but with the proper pruning and a soaking now and then with her prize cow manure "tea," she might get twice-a-year bloom.

She wiped the blood off the telephone with her shirt-tail and resolutely turned her back on the door leading to the backyard. Allowing for time to get lost, Edge should be there within the hour. She left her sneakers under the kitchen table and took big steps through the living room to avoid smearing the waxed pine boards of the floor and the rag rugs she had that morning vigorously shaken dust and dog hair out of in the sun and breeze. At least the room would look clean to the company. The old basket full of brilliant zinnias and marigolds looked gaudy as a Mardi Gras parade on the pine two-board kitchen table.

She supposed she should make some iced tea—or would they want beer or whiskey? She didn't stock much of either and she didn't have time to make a run to the store. Tea it would have to be. She took big steps back into the kitchen, put on the teakettle, fished out a family-sized tea bag, and put it in the blue crockery pitcher that had been her grandmother's. Fortunately it was too late for lunch and too early for supper, so she could get by with crackers and cheese.

The loft bedroom was small. The pitch of the cabin roof slanting from the narrow ceiling to the eaves left little headroom for tall people and space for only low furniture. But it had been comfortable enough for her and Benjy and after his death she lay in the old rope bed and stared at the rafters wondering how long she could stand the cabin—or life itself—without him. The passage of the years had helped; now she felt encompassed in warmth and safety by the slanting walls. As she zipped herself into a clean skirt and shirt, she looked at the little bedroom with love and gratitude. The red-brown pine rafters caught the afternoon light through the narrow, small-paned windows, and the old quilt that served her as a spread picked it up in the main bright points of the Star of the East pattern.

She sat in the low sewing rocker to put on her clean sneakers and let her eyes travel over the pictures that covered the top of the old chestnut washstand: Benjy in his faded blue running suit with a dark eyebrow lifted quizzically; her father many years before his death, proud in his policeman's uniform with his captain's gold bars and the badge on his cap still bright in the old black and white snapshot; her mother, slim and pretty in their courtship days, wearing a cloche hat and the short skirt of the flapper era; a snapshot of her two little neighbors, Sheena and Kim Sue Gandy, when they were small enough to be loaded in a red wagon and towed by Benjy behind the lawn mower.

A half-finished oil painting of Kate in a droopy cotton

bathing suit occupied the bathroom wall, the contribution of a nonartistic friend from the newspaper who painted it one summer afternoon when a group of them gathered at Kate and Benjy's cabin for what they called "culcha and collation," which meant homemade art and a picnic by a neighbor's pond. Only one or two had any training, but they staged a contest and everybody entered it. The picture of Kate, executed by the obit editor, won third place. She was standing with her legs apart peering into the depths of the murky pond water, looking, Benjy had observed, like she had just peed.

Another picture, said to be an abstract, amused Kate because it reminded her of her cat Sugar and her dog Pepper in a fight. The artist called it "Crisis in Sopchoppy," and Kate hung it over the dresser facing her bed to toughen her when she started out in the morning for whatever crisis her day held.

Towers of books teetered and toppled from her bedside table, from her dresser, and from stacks along the wall. They were library books and books to review for the paper and finds at yard sales. One wall of the living room was covered with shelves full of "keepers," but until she arrived at a verdict on a book, Kate did not shelve it.

A basket of daisies from her yard hid bottles and jars on her dresser top, and Kate wondered if she had time to collect another bouquet for the old ironstone chamber pot in the bathroom. A roar on the road distracted her and she went to the window in time to see a wrecker truck pull in her driveway with an ancient rust-eroded Chevrolet in tow behind it.

She made it to the back steps in time to see a woman

and two men get out of the cab of the truck. One man she knew, Dipstick Jenkins of the Roswell Bring 'em Back Alive Wrecker and Towing Service.

"Hi, Dip!" she called. "What did you bring me?"

"Kinfolks, Kate," he said, wiping the grease from his hands on the seat of his khaki pants and walking toward her. "And their chariot," waving toward the battered and beat-up car. "Where you want it?"

Want it? Kate said to herself. *Out of my yard, of course.* But she sensed that it went with her visitors, the man and a woman she thought at a glance could be a dead ringer for Tammie Bakker, plump with gilt hair and pink- and blue-enameled lips, cheeks, and eyes.

They came toward her, arms outstretched for hugs. And she, who liked to reserve hugs for honest affection for children and old friends, let them envelop her and even hugged them back.

"Edge," she said. "And this must be Bambi! I'm glad to see you," but glancing at the wrecker, "I'm sorry you had to arrive this way. Did your car break down?"

"You could say that," said Edge ruefully. "Fortunately right in front of this fellow's place."

Kate searched his short chunky frame and his red face for some resemblance to Benjy. A straw version of a Dallas Cowboys cheerleader's ten-gallon hat covered his entire head except for two long mustard-colored sideburns, and he did not take it off even for introductions. It was hard to tell what he really looked like.

"Well, come in," Kate said, and then, remembering the boiling teakettle, "I'll fix us some tea. You too, Dip. I appreciate your bringing them. Can you fix their car?"

"It's not that, Kate," said the garage man uneasily.

"They couldn't pay, so I thought this"—he waved toward the old car—"was best. I'll unhitch and run on back to the shop. Take you up on your tea some other day."

If they couldn't pay for repairs, Kate wondered, what about the tow—seven or eight miles at least? Didn't Dip charge for that?

Edge answered her unspoken question by rummaging vainly in his pants pockets. "We seem to be out of cash and Mr. Jenkins here wouldn't take a traveler's check," he said at last.

From the look of surprise on Dip's face, Kate thought it was the first he had heard of the traveler's checks.

"Well, wait a minute," she said. "Let me get my pocketbook. How much, Dip?"

"Twenty-five," Dip said uncomfortably.

When Kate got back with her purse, Edge and Bambi were lifting suitcases from the tow truck and the trunk of their car. They lined them up by the driveway and Kate looked at them in chagrin. Neat expensive cases, she guessed, but so many of them!

She remembered Benjy's joke when an old friend from the Marines came to spend the night with more than one bag.

"Good God, fellow," he had cried, "how long you intend to stay?"

How long did this garish couple intend to stay?

The state of their car gave her pause. If it wasn't repaired, they probably couldn't go. She turned to Dip.

"Did you see what ails the car?"

"Everything, just about," he said, grinning. "But the alternator is what caused it to quit."

"Is that bad?" asked Kate, glancing at Edge, who

seemed very busy rearranging the lineup of suitcases in the yard.

"We-ell, all things considered," said Dip.

"Never mind talking like National Public Radio," said Kate briskly, referring to her favorite afternoon listening program. "Go on and fix the whatchmacallit and we'll worry about the bill when the time comes. Just call me."

Edge and Bambi gave no sign that they were a party to this transaction or had heard any of it. They stood by their disabled car and looked hungrily at the rooftops of the subdivision mansions that were visible beyond the thicket that bordered Kate's front yard, past the dirt road and green belt of woodland left by the builders.

"Nice," said Edge. "Who lives over there?"

"Oh, that's the subdivision," Kate said. "By now there are lots of people over there, maybe a couple of dozen. I don't know many of them. When we moved here, it was all woods with just a little trail to the river where we liked to walk."

"I like that flesh-colored stucco," Bambi broke a shy silence to offer.

Kate craned her neck to follow Bambi's gaze. The back wall of a two-story stucco glowed rosily through a stand of pines.

"That's the Dunns'," Kate said. "You may meet them. I know them a little better than most of the new people because they had a meeting at their house about the dirt road and I went."

"Hey, you gon' git it paved?" said Dip in a congratulatory tone.

Kate scowled at him. "Not if I can help it. They have plenty of paved streets and sidewalks and gutters over there. They better leave my peaceful old road alone!"

Dip laughed disbelievingly and Edge and Bambi turned their attention to the log cabin. They had picked up some of their suitcases and were staring appraisingly at the old walls.

Kate, following their glance, was pleased with the picture the house made in the late afternoon sun. The old logs, part pine and part oak and chestnut, were not uniformly silver but struck here and there with a dash of ocher borrowed from the summer sun and shadowed by the deep gray of winter storms. She had a fancy that the undaubed spaces between the logs captured and held moonlight, and she knew from experience that they admitted sleet and snow when winter came.

Dip maneuvered his tow truck to get the decrepit Chevrolet out on the gravel road, touched his siren briefly, flicked on his dome light, waved jauntily, and was gone.

Kate looked over at Edge and Bambi and said cordially, "That's it—my famous log cabin. It's a hundred and fifty years old now. Do you like it?"

"Super," said Edge.

Bambi looked as if she might cry. Her painted jowls sagged and her blue eye shadow looked suspiciously damp. "How big is it?" she asked dolefully.

"Oh, not big," said Kate lightly. "But big enough for one person. Since Benjy died, I practically rattle around in it. However, the man who built it had twelve children and I understand they managed."

The minute she said it, she was sorry. She knew that without a doubt she was going to have to manage with at least two more people. On impulse she said suddenly, "Do you all have any children?"

Bambi brightened momentarily. "One. A son. He's twelve and he's supposed to come as soon as . . ." She faltered and looked at Edge.

"Yeah, we're sending him bus fare," Edge said grandly. "As soon as I find work."

Kate directed the visitors to leave their luggage on the back porch and led them to the weathered cypress chairs under the maple tree. It was an old trick to speed guests—keep them outside so they can't dig in and stay long. But she knew it wouldn't work this time because obviously the Greens had no place to go and no way of getting there, what with their car being dragged by the scruff of the neck to the garage.

To mend her manners, she said it was cooler in the yard, a nice little breeze that didn't prevail in the cabin. "Has it been a hot summer in Texas?" she asked.

Edge nodded. "Record-breaking," he said.

"But, hon, you know we had air-conditioning," put in Bambi, eyeing the cabin suspiciously. "You got air-conditioning in there?"

"Ah, no," said Kate. "Log walls have a lot of natural insulation. It's been fairly comfortable even on the hot days."

"Why you got that kind of house?" asked Bambi, wrinkling her nose just a little and then rallying. "Even if it is cute."

"I don't really know," confessed Kate, laughing. "Benjy and I liked it and I guess I still do."

"Well, I'm looking forward to seeing the inside," said Edge.

"Oh, sure," said Kate. "I'm sorry to park you here. Maybe you want to change your clothes or something and visit the bathroom. Come on in. While I get our iced tea you all can take the tour. With only three rooms you don't have to have a guide."

She steered them and their mountain of suitcases into the living room and was a little jolted to see them climbing the stairs with all their stuff in hand.

The room wouldn't hold it! But where else could they put their luggage? She filled the tea glasses with ice and sliced a lemon and set out a plate of crackers and cheese. She put it all on a tray and carried it to the backyard.

When the Greens finally came outside, they had already changed into shorts and T-shirts. Bambi had evidently been admonished about the proper appreciation of the cabin.

"So darling, Kate! The darlingest little house I ever saw—and so many old things. Just like my grandma had, quilts and everything!"

"Thank you," said Kate dryly. "I hope you all will plan to spend the night with me."

The way they looked at one another she knew they were thinking *Where else?* but they said they'd love to and fell on the crackers and cheese as if they hadn't eaten in days. *Poor things, they're hungry,* thought Kate. *I should be thinking about something for supper.*

She had planned on a fat juicy tomato sandwich for herself with the tomatoes that were flourishing in her tiny garden. Ripe peaches, all rose and gold and dripping honey, were falling from the trees at the edge of the yard. She could make a shortcake. Would it be enough?

"Where did you eat lunch?" she asked.

"To tell the truth, we were in such a rush to get here we didn't stop," Edge said.

"Cheese crackers and a Coke somewhere in Alabama," Bambi said drearily, eyeing the plate on the table.

"Oh, well, we'll do better than that." Kate faked a cheerfulness she didn't feel. She could run in to the grocery store, she supposed, and get red meat and potatoes, but she didn't want to. It was, after all, her day off.

"We don't want to put no burden on you," Edge said. "It's just that . . . well, you've heard how bad things got in Texas with the oil recession and all. I was working in Houston and I lost my job. Hung around two years and used up all we had, including our house."

"And my good car," said Bambi. "Lincoln Town Car, it was."

"No work anywhere," went on Edge. "I happened to remember you and Benjy and I thought, you know, family and all. So here we are."

"You're very welcome," said Kate warmly, standing up to go in the house and check the larder.

At that moment she heard her dog Pepper barking playfully in the front yard and the voice of her old neighbor, Miss Willie Wilcox, hailing her with a country "Hey-o!"

Kate went to meet her as she came around the corner of the house. Pepper was frolicking beside her with a tongue-lolling skittishness that was unexpected in an old dog, except that he counted Miss Willie as his special friend and sometime guardian when Kate had to be away from home. She was an old country woman, in her mid-eighties, and had been a resident of what they called "the Cove" since she arrived as a young girl to marry an old widower named Cy Wilcox who had a motherless son and a good-sized farm down by the creek. She and Kate had become close friends and when the Wilcox land was divided up and sold by Garney Wilcox, Miss Willie's stepson, to developers for a subdivision, Miss Willie and Kate were drawn even closer together. Garney had put the old lady in a nursing home and then he himself was found dead in her house. Kate had flatly refused to believe in the old lady's guilt and events subsequently proved she was right. Now Miss Willie was living happily in the old gray weathered house in the woods on the other side of the subdivision, and had resumed her time-honored role as everybody's best neighbor.

She had a basket on her arm today and Kate peered at it hopefully. Provender for supper?

"Lord, you got company," Miss Willie said, "and here I come in my old fishing rags."

Kate made introductions and was glad to see Edge get to his feet. Bambi started to extend her hand and then, evidently smelling the contents of the basket, withdrew it.

"You all like fish?" asked Miss Willie.

"Yes, ma'am!" said Edge eagerly. Bambi didn't reply.

"My old rooster was crowing for company today," Miss Willie said, "and since it ain't my company, I figgered it must be your'n, Kate. So you git the ketch! Six of the finest bream I've caught all summer."

Kate took the basket and peered in. Scaled and gutted and fine without question.

"Miss Willie, you're a godsend," she said. "I was wondering what to cook for supper and you settled it for me. Come in and eat with us!"

"No, I'm much obliged," Miss Willie said. "I got my feeding up to do."

Kate laughed.

"Miss Willie talks like she still has livestock—milking

and hay to pitch down for a mule," she said to the Greens. "She used to have all that—but what are you 'feeding up' now, Miss Willie?"

The older woman laughed. "Not much," she admitted. "My chickens and a cat or two. This time a day hit's mostly watering my flower beds and garden stuff."

She turned the talk from herself back to the Greens. "I reckon I'll be seeing you'uns later? You planning to stay a spell, ain't you?"

Edge looked hopefully at Kate.

Bambi pointedly looked away.

Miss Willie realized the matter had not yet been settled. And Kate, beginning to feel trapped, didn't want to commit herself with an excess of cordiality. She got around it by changing the subject.

"I'll walk you a ways," she said to Miss Willie, and to Edge and Bambi, "Back in a minute. Have some more tea."

She set the basket of fish on the porch and followed Miss Willie to the edge of the yard, where the gate opened onto the dirt road. Ahead of her, Miss Willie opened the gate and turned to face Kate, her dark eyes rebuking her.

"They needful, ain't they?" She nodded toward the couple under the tree in the backyard.

"I'm afraid so," said Kate.

"Well, remember your scripture," she said sternly. "Spread out your hands to the poor, reach for the needy."

For a woman who had so little schooling and could barely read or write, Miss Willie had an amazing ability to recall scripture when she needed it.

"I bet I know," Kate teased, giving her old neighbor a

hug. "You're back on that virtuous woman in the Bible, aren't you?"

"Hit's a right tolerable place to be," Miss Willie admitted, grinning. "You and me both best try."

"Aw, okay," Kate said, "and thank you for the fish. I'll fry them for supper right away. I do believe the Greens are hungry."

Miss Willie nodded and crossed the road, taking the path through the woods beyond. Kate turned back toward her guests. *I can quote, too,* she said silently to Miss Willie: *"A poor relation is the most irrelevant thing in nature." Charles Lamb.* It made her feel better and more tolerant of her visitors. She hurried to collect Miss Willie's basket of bream and headed for the kitchen.

She did feel a little ashamed that she was not more welcoming. She hoped she had not revealed any lack of warmth to Edge and Bambi because they were, after all, Benjy's kin. He had been a totally hospitable person, welcoming all friends, any relations, and even strangers. If they happened to be "needful," as Miss Willie put it, he was all the more cordial, having grown up, as Kate herself had, in the years of the Depression when "haves" were obliged to share with "have-nots."

Police pensions were small when she was a child, and she remembered the procession of old retired officer friends who passed through their house, sometimes taking Kate's bed, leaving her to sleep on a pallet on the floor as befitted, her father had said, young bones. There was always a place at the table for anybody who came, and Kate remembered that sometimes supplies ran out, although that was before her father was disabled in a shootout with a robber, and was bringing home a paycheck. The money seemed to run out before the month did, but when there wasn't money for pork chops and sweet potatoes, they ate collards out of her father's small garden; if the garden was not producing, there was always a feast of hot biscuits and cane syrup.

Though this turned the child Kate against biscuits and syrup, her appetite for them had returned with the passage of years. Now she rolled Miss Willie's fish in cornmeal and waited for the fat in her iron skillet to heat and thought she might give her guests biscuits and syrup for breakfast. After all, Benjy had always said her biscuits were food for the gods.

Kate smiled to herself and went to the door to check on the Greens. They were wandering over the yard and had reached the little vegetable plot where tomatoes made a nice show but little else flourished, except a few herbs and possibly a row of radishes.

She filled her grits pot and set it to boil and surveyed the dishes in the old pie safe that served as a china cabinet. She loved dishes and through the years had collected some pretty ones. Day in and day out her mother's old dime-store Fiesta ware suited her, but now she reached for the Franciscan dogwood pottery and pale green linen place mats, which pleased her by matching the colors in the plates.

The water boiled and Kate hurried to sift the creamy grain into the pot, stirring it gently as it submerged. Maybe the Greens didn't like grits with their fish. Nowadays a lot of people didn't like grits. But these were from Texas and wasn't that big state in the grits belt? In case they weren't grits enthusiasts, Kate added a lump of butter and a dollop of cream and a dust of cayenne to the pot.

As she went to the door to call the Greens, they reached the back steps.

"Supper's about ready," she said. "I didn't think to ask you earlier, but would you like something to drink? A beer or some of my scuppernong wine?"

Bambi started to speak, but Edge cut her off.

"No, ma'am!" he said emphatically. "We don't imbibe."

He looked warningly at Bambi, who looked back sulkily. Suddenly, apparently gathering a measure of defiance, she made a liar of him. "I would. I'll take a beer."

Edge glared at her but apparently let himself be diverted by three deep red silken-skinned tomatoes he held in his hands.

"All right to pick these?" he asked. "I couldn't resist."

"I'm glad you brought them," Kate said. "I hadn't thought of a salad. I have some green onions and the last of the leaf lettuce from the garden. You know how fast it goes when the hot weather hits us."

"Sure do," Edge said. "I left the farm early, but I remember my mama and papa's fight with that old Texas dirt."

"Are they still in Beeville?" Kate asked.

"They passed away," Edge said, heading for the bathroom before Kate had time for an expression of sympathy.

Bambi, flipping the top off a beer can, looked after him and made a face. "He don't like to talk about them," she said, taking a gulp of her beer. "And I don't blame him. Poor as pig shit. Kinda like your neighbor, Miss Willard, or whatever her name is."

"It's Miss Willie," Kate said, "and I don't believe you can call her poor. She has land and a good sound house and . . ." She paused. What Miss Willie had wouldn't impress this fool woman, who may have been given that name at birth but sure had time to change it. Miss Willie really didn't have much in the way of worldly goods. But Kate had never thought of her as poor. Her pleasure in the earth and her knowledge of it, her kindness and generosity, her wisdom made her seem rich. "She's like David," she finally said, "full of days and riches and honor."

"Like who?" Bambi asked.

Kate stirred the grits and pretended not to hear. She did not expect a bit of Old Testament to make a dent in the hazy mind that lay back of that badly dyed head.

"Oh, a friend of yours," Bambi said, smirking triumphantly. "A boyfriend."

Kate smiled, nodded, tore up the lettuce, and skinned the tomatoes.

"You can put out the napkins," she said, nodding toward the old jam cupboard which held table linens.

"Sure," said Bambi. She opened the red buttermilk-stained door and peered in. "Good gawd," she said. "You got 'em, ain't you? Don't you use paper?"

"Not if I can help it," Kate said. "Cloth napkins are easy to wash and I enjoy pressing them. Some of those were my mother's, some my grandmother's, some I've picked up here and there, mostly at yard sales. Get three green ones."

"If you say so," said Bambi. "Mind if I have another beer? This hard labor makes me thirsty."

"Help yourself," Kate said, just as Edge came back from washing up.

"No," he said quietly but firmly. "One's enough." And then, attempting a smile, "We don't want to drink up

Cuz'n Kate's supply. If she should get thirsty, we mighty far out in the country and our car—"

"Whose fault is that?" whined Bambi. "I told you we should have kept the Lincoln. Leaving town they'd never have caught us."

"That would have been dishonest," Edge said with what Kate felt was false piety.

Bambi must have thought so, too. She laughed merrily and reached for another beer.

Miss Willie's bream were so fresh they curled when they hit the hot skillet and so tender Edge and Bambi picked them up with their fingers and ate greedily until the platter was empty. Kate held back to give them a chance. They did not dig into the grits and she wondered about their raising. Texans and no grits with their fish? There are parts of Tennessee, she had been told, where people reject the southern mainstay of ground corn. Being a big state, Texas was home to all kinds.

Kate cleaned up the kitchen with minimal help from Edge. Bambi had refinished the enamel and gloss on her face and wandered out toward the road.

"Looking for your neighbors or traffic on the road," Edge explained indulgently. "She's young and city-raised."

"Well, there are a lot of people over there." Kate nodded toward the subdivision beyond the dirt road and the thicket of small trees and bushes she had grown as a screen. She wiped out her iron skillet and set it in the oven to dry. "I don't know all of them. Just Miss Willie, who was here about a hundred years before Benjy and I found this place. She likes the neighbors and I'm sure I would, too, if I had time for visiting, but I go into town to work every day. And when I'm at home I seem to have a lot to do."

"Yeah," said Edge, "you got a lot on your hands. While me and Bambi are here, you can put us to work. Anything you want done in the house or the yard, we'll be glad to do it."

Kate winced inwardly. It sounded like a long siege. She really didn't want any help in keeping the old log cabin and its yard. Once a year a farmer from up near Little River came by and plowed her garden for her and brought her a load of cow manure. Most times she took pleasure in managing the old log structure she and Benjy had found and restored twenty years ago. She glanced at the log walls. Obviously there was dust there, a gray velvety fuzz, and on some of the old blue and gray graniteware pans and kettles she had picked up through the years before they became what was now called "collectibles." She lovingly took them down and washed them once a year, but it was not anything she felt pressured about. After all, the dust had been there for a century or more and, as she had loved to tell Benjy when he mentioned it, it had never hurt anybody yet.

She smiled at Edge. "You are kind to offer, but I really like to take care of this little place myself. There's not much to it."

"Well, how about the yard?" he asked "You got a lawn mower, I see, out there in the shed. And the grass."

"Yeah, I guess it needs cutting. I always delay. Maybe it's laziness, but I tell myself I don't want to cut all the good plants that grow up in the grass. Daffodils and violets in the spring and sometimes bluets and wild strawberries. A lot of wild plants—butterfly weed and purple heal-all and Venus lookinglass and Jersey tea. They were all here when I came and I don't want to run them off."

Unlike some people, she added to herself.

Edge smiled tolerantly and handed her the dish towel. "I'll go out yonder and see what Miss Bambi is up to."

Kate went upstairs to put clean sheets on the bed. She was stunned by the amount of disorder that two people and their luggage could wreak in a couple of hours. Suitcases were open, spilling out underwear and running suits and bright-colored sandals and sneakers and boots. She stumbled over a makeup case before she saw it and knocked a conglomeration of bottles and tubes and little boxes to the floor. Rubbing her instep, which had struck the metal corner of the red-and-gold-brocade case, she limped to the linen closet and stood looking and marveling at how their possessions had overwhelmed her small but ordinarily starkly neat room.

She decided not to touch the mélange. She put two sheets and two pillowcases on the foot of the bed, found another set for herself, took her nightgown and robe out of the closet, and went back downstairs.

She would let them make up their own bed—if they could get to it. She would open out the sofa in the living room and make it up for herself, hoping her guests would take the hint and let her go to bed early. Not that she would sleep, but she had a stack of books she wanted to get to and if she pleaded sleep they might go upstairs and settle in themselves.

Darkness began to fall on the little cabin and its disorderly yard when the Greens came back. Kate had turned on the yard light, a dim electric bulb in an old farm lantern that she had attached to a branch of the persimmon tree at the edge of the driveway, just enough light, she had long ago decided, to steer a visitor to the cabin and to illuminate any creepy-crawly creatures that might be on the path when she drove in at night. She kept it purposely dim because she did not want to capitulate to the pressure for streetlights and floodlights that the subdivision fostered. A little light was a good thing, but too much light destroyed the illusion that she was in the country and dimmed the brilliance of the moon and stars.

The Greens didn't agree.

"Cuz, you need a brighter light out yonder," Edge said when he and Bambi walked into the kitchen where Kate, as a guilty afterthought, had set cinnamon buns to rise for breakfast instead of the staple biscuits. It was a routine rite for expected company. Why couldn't she manage a little preparation for these unexpected guests? She had the buns rolled and cut and sprinkled with brown sugar and cinnamon when the two walked in.

"Ugh!" cried Bambi, sniffing the air. "You cooking something with cinnamon in it!"

"Something good, shug," said Edge hastily. "Cuz'n Kate is treating us mighty fine."

He gave Bambi a little push toward the stairs. "Why don't you get ready for nighty-night?"

Good Lord, Kate thought, *going to bed is now going to be "nighty-night" in this humble old cabin.*

"As I was saying," Edge resumed, "that's not much of a light you got out there. When I get my car—*if* I get my car—I've got some electric wire and some floodlights and I'll put you in something uptown, even better than them people across the road."

"Well, thank you," said Kate absently. No use trying to explain that she didn't want any better, "uptown" lighting system. Besides, she was struck by the fact that he had said *if* he got his car back. It might be possible that it was beyond repair and he knew it.

The possibility stuck in her mind, even after the Greens had gone to bed and she had settled herself on the sofa with a book and a reading light. If they didn't have a car, what then? Would they be her guests forever? She turned out the light and listened to their voices overhead. Bambi seemed to be crying and Edge was making soothing sounds to shush her. Poor things, Kate thought. Needful, as Miss Willie had said. She had so much that she shouldn't be grudging about sharing some of it with them. For a while.

Kate reproached herself with something she had read by an old writer named Jeremy Taylor. She was being, as he had deplored, "in love with sorrow and peevishness" and chose by her worrying to sit down upon her "little handful of thorns."

She closed her eyes and fought for sleep.

The sweet rolls, smelling uncompromisingly of cinnamon, were eaten, even by Bambi, who came to the table in a short nightgown and a lacy peignoir.

Kate, dressed for work in a coffee-colored linen suit with brown and white spectator pumps, scribbled her office number on a notepad and, as an afterthought, added the garage number of Dipstick Jenkins.

"You might call him a little bit later," Kate said to Edge. "Call me and let me know what he says. If it isn't too much I can spring for the garage bill."

"That'll be super," said Edge, reaching for the last cinnamon roll. "You go ahead to your job. Me and Bambi will do the dishes."

Kate thanked them and headed for the yard. First to feed her cat Sugar and her dog Pepper, who had been receptive to the guests but not overly friendly. Pepper, chomping away on his dried food, stopped to look over his shoulder toward the couple in the kitchen as if to say, *You're not leaving them here in my hands, are you?*

Kate patted them both reassuringly and took her customary morning turn around the yard. She had been struggling for several years to establish a cottage garden at the cabin door. Larkspur and poppies had done so well in the spring they had given her false hope. Too much shade and too much dry weather had reacted discouragingly on the happy roundelay of blooming annuals and perennials she had hoped to have. She could count on four o'clocks in the late afternoon—reliable, unpretentious four o'clocks. The moonflowers had stayed quiescent, an unprepossessing green vine that climbed to the top of the rough trellis over the cabin door. Only in the last few weeks, to her surprise and delight, had they decided to bloom. At sunset they unfurled their silken snowy white umbrellas with their delicate ribs of green, looking silvery in the early twilight. In the early morning light there were still a few flowers closing slowly, and the sight cheered Kate.

There's hope, she thought, *it will all come around one day, even the ginger lilies*—which a minister friend had given her and which adamantly refused to bloom. She checked them daily, hopefully sniffing at the air in case one fragrant bract of white bloom might be hidden under a clump of daisies or a rose in the humble little patch.

What she smelled was two grubby hands over her eyes.

"Guess who!" cried a giggling twelve-year-old.

"A Gandy," said Kate.

"Which one?" demanded the voice behind the hands.

"Sheena!" guessed Kate, pushing the hands away and turning.

"Yah, yah, yah!" cried the two girls in unison. "It was Kim Sue. You guessed wrong!"

"You're getting so big," Kate smiled, hugging them both. "I didn't expect you to reach my eyes so easily. Come on in and meet my company. Mr. Benjy's cousins from Texas. I've got to get to the office and you might entertain them for me."

Just as Edge and Bambi in her frothy nightclothes came out onto the porch, Miss Willie called from the front yard.

"Oh, Miss Willie." Kate went to meet her. "Your fish were wonderful. We ate them for supper last night and they were just great."

Miss Willie nodded distractedly. "It's Mr. Renty, Kate. He's done took off again. His niece lives over the river is a-looking! Says she's gon' have him locked up this time."

"Aw, no," said Kate.

"Cain't you do something?" Miss Willie asked worriedly. "He's plumb sweet on you since you give him leave to eat all your blueberries."

Kate smiled, remembering. The old gentleman had thumbed a ride with her from up at Chadwick's store one day years ago. He was very old, child-small, with diminutive hands and feet, snow-white hair, and a pink face that reminded Kate of a little billy goat she had had when they first moved to the country. His blue eyes held the merry light of a wise child. She had offered to take him home, wherever that was, but his eyes had fallen on her blueberry bushes, heavy and sweet under their ripening crop.

"Home?" he had said vaguely. "I ain't got a homeplace no more. Oncet I had me a homestead with the best blueberries in the settlement. Air them as sweet as them look?"

"I don't know," Kate said. "But you are welcome to pick them and try. I'll give you a bowl."

"No bowl needed," the old man said, grinning impishly. "I'll pick into my pockets."

"That'll ruin your clothes, turn 'em blue," Kate objected.

"Blue's true!" said the old man, laughing a childish "hoo hoo."

Kate had meant to get a bowl anyhow, but when she got in the cabin and put up her groceries, the phone was ringing and half an hour had passed before she returned to the blueberry bushes and Mr. Renty with a bowl.

At first she didn't see him; then she heard him chirping like a bird. He was sitting in a sort of makeshift tent he had wriggled out in the weeds and grass beneath the blueberry bushes, eating out of his shirt pocket, which was bulging with berries and was, in truth, dyed blue.

Kate offered him the bowl, which he took and put on his head like a World War I soldier's helmet.

"Now, Mr. Renty, if you're not gon' pick into it, you'd better give me back my bowl," Kate wheedled.

"Nope," said the old man, pulling himself out of his briary little nest. "I'm a-going and I thank you kindly for berries and bowl."

Kate thought she would never forget the picture of the

little man dancing down the middle of the dirt road with her best yellow mixing bowl inverted over his dandelion fluff of hair.

She had seen him a few times after that, always when he flagged her on the road and jauntily commandeered her vehicle for a ride to Chadwick's store, Ebenezer Church, or some house in the area. He never mentioned the bowl, but he would ask if her blueberries were "ready" and when she brought him up to date he would say, "Them's good berries. I'll be back."

He came at odd seasons, usually when she was not at home. He picked whatever fruit and berries were ripe, filling his pockets and loping off.

Miss Willie had remembered an old family place "foot of yan mountain," but she wasn't sure if he still lived there. "You best quit picking him up," she once warned Kate. "He's bad to run away and you're a-heping him."

Kate had laughed. At least she had never taken him far enough to count.

"Oh, I think it's fine for him to go where he pleases, Miss Willie," she had said. "It's good to see such independence."

"It ain't good when he gits out at night and goes," Miss Willie protested. "Last time somebody nearabout run over him walking down the middle of the big paved road, so his niece said."

That did give Kate pause, and she promised not to give him any more rides. But then she hadn't seen him since. Now he had apparently run away again.

"If you was to find him somers," Miss Willie pointed out, "he would git in the car with you. He might run from a stranger."

It was true. Kate could see him skittish as a young chicken taking off, white hair blowing in the breeze, maybe still wearing her yellow bowl at a tilt.

"Okay, Miss Willie. I'll take a turn around the settlement. I better call the office first."

"Kin we go with you?" asked Kim Sue.

"Go ask your mother," Kate said, "while I make a phone call and change my shoes." If the search involved walking over rocky slopes and down steep riverbanks, she did not want to be wearing her best heels. She thought of calling the county police but remembered that they wouldn't wage a search unless somebody had been missing for a couple of weeks—and knowing Mr. Renty's reputation, they probably wouldn't look for him at all.

"Where's his niece?" Kate asked Miss Willie.

"Lord, I don't know," the old woman said. "She come drivin' by my house first day. Said he'd been gone the longest time and I reckon now she's gone to make arrangements."

Kate was startled. Making "arrangements" sounded funereal.

"She thinks he's dead?"

Miss Willie laughed. "Not death arrangements. Arrangements to put him in the insane asylum."

"Worse than death," Kate muttered. As a reporter she had known the state's mental institutions when they provided living death for many patients. They had undergone major improvements, but still she didn't want her fey friend locked up. "If that's what his niece is gon' do, I'm not looking for Mr. Renty. Let him stay free. He's not crazy."

"Oh, Cuz, I can't agree with you," said Edge from the

steps. He had not spoken before except to wave or smile at Miss Willie and acknowledge Kate's introduction to the Gandy sisters. "Sounds definitely off." He tapped his temple officiously.

"Sounds screwy to me," Bambi offered.

"No," said Kate, annoyed. "He just marches to a different drummer."

"Well, I hope he's not marching around here," said Bambi, shivering and glancing apprehensively into the woods that encircled the cabin.

Just then, Kim Sue and Sheena came galloping back from their house. "Aw, he ain't gon' rape you," Sheena assured Bambi. "He's too old."

"Thanks, Sheena," Kate said dryly, acknowledging the support. She didn't have to ask her thirteen-year-old neighbor where she had learned about rape. She was educated about sex crimes, as were all her contemporaries, by watching television. The Gandys, descendants of an old country family, had given up hog killing, square dancing, and candy pulls as forms of recreation and spent twelve hours a day watching television.

"Aw, Kate," protested Miss Willie, "you do the best you kin to hep the old feller and leave the results up to the Lord. He may be sick or hurt out yan somers, and ain't nobody but you to hep him."

"How about his niece?" asked Kate grumpily. "I should start with her. She must be concerned about him to be out looking."

"Oh, we know why she's a-looking," put in Sheena.

"Our mommer says she's got a feller wants her to git Mr. Renty's house so they can live in it themselves. Mommer says Charlie—that's her name—is tard of working up there at the Dairy Queen and wants to git married. It's easier if you got proppity."

"No doubt," said Kate.

Miss Willie looked reproving. "You don't know that for a fack, little Gandy, and hit don't become you to talk about grown folks' business."

"No, it doesn't," Kate concurred. "But if it should be true . . . poor Mr. Renty. Is it his place she's trying to get?"

"Reckon it is," said Miss Willie. "A tolerable stout old house across the river. I reckon it was deeded to him by his mommer and papa, but he ain't spent much time living in it. Too busy road-walking."

"Well, get in the car, Sheena and Kim Sue, if your mama said you can go. Edge, Bambi, do you want to join the search? Miss Willie?"

The Greens said they would stay by the phone and wait to hear about their car. Miss Willie said she had her Monday washing to get on the line but would be glad to put her foot in the road if Kate needed her.

Kate drove down to the paved road and through the Shining Waters subdivision. She didn't think it likely that Mr. Renty would be there, but it was a start. What had once been pine woods with one old wagon road leading to the river when she and Benjy had first moved into the cabin were now paved streets lined with handsome half-million-dollar houses representing every kind of architecture Kate had ever seen, with the exception of log cabins and sharecroppers' shacks. There were French chalets, half-timbered stucco and brick, clapboard, and some new building material that Kate couldn't peg, but considered nonetheless splendid. She had never dreamed her own forest would be felled to make way for swimming pools and tennis courts and cunning little gazebos. She and Miss Willie had laughed together when the little stream called Shine Creek (because it had served generations of moonshiners) became Shining Waters in developer-ese and gave its name to the subdivision.

Kate was now used to the subdivision and had several acquaintances who lived there. Once there had been an obnoxious young couple who were involved in drug trafficking and murder, but she had helped to see them into the state penitentiary.

The remaining population, she believed, were not only affluent, but friendly, law-abiding, well-mannered people. However, she did not think they were likely to offer refuge to Mr. Renty or that he would visit them. For one thing, they had blooming shrubs and fine trees but no blueberry bushes.

Even as Kate thought of blueberries, Kim Sue had an idea.

"You know, Miss Kate, apples is ripening up on Mr. Banana Pierce's old field—and Mr. Renty liked to gether fruit."

Kate had always enjoyed being "nigh neighbor," as Miss Willie called it, to the old home site of a man called "Mr. Banana." He had been a produce peddler in the days when such entrepreneurs were rare in the farming country, and, best of all, he brought to them from the coast, rarest of all in an inland area, that golden fruit of the gods, bananas. Of such was his fame born. Mr. Banana Pierce had died years before Kate had moved to the country, and the house he had lived in was gone. But the field and a dooryard, which sustained things he and Mrs. Pierce had planted, attracted her often. She especially liked to be there in the spring when his crabapple trees bloomed, and there was a thorny shrub that had been used in an effort to graft orange trees, apparently a dream of Mr. Banana's. It had fragrant orange blossomlike blooms in the spring and hard, bitter fruit in late summer. Mr. Banana must have learned that he couldn't grow oranges in northern Georgia, but the thorny bush flourished. Several times a year Kate visited it for flowers and its strange bitter fruit, and at Christmastime to get stickery branches to turn into gumdrop trees for the children of friends.

She had forgotten the old sour apple tree toward the back of the yard and she smiled at Kim Sue gratefully.

"You have a good idea," she said. "Wouldn't it be wonderful if we found him picking apples?"

She parked on the road out of sight of the backyard in case Mr. Renty was watching and might take off. She and the girls climbed the barbed-wire fence and walked quietly through a fine growth of Queen Anne's lace and blackberry briars.

The apple tree, old and gnarled, its trunk patterned with lacy gray-green lichens, had apparently been visited—and recently. There were no apples on the lower branches, but a few freckled ones hung on near the top. Beneath, the tree leaves had been swept into a pile, perhaps to make a bed, Kate thought, and the soil where they had been was soft enough to retain tracks—the little tracks of a child-sized man.

Kate and the Gandy sisters exchanged triumphant looks.

"Let's follow the tracks," she whispered, and Kim Sue took her hand as Sheena nodded vigorously.

The tracks led down a slope toward the spring under the big oak tree—a spot Kate and Benjy had discovered for themselves years before and adopted for picnics. It was a small spring, probably now filled with leaves and pinestraw and dirt washing down the hill in the years since Mrs. Banana kept her milk and butter there. But it made a pleasant sound, was cooling to the feet of waders, and was haven to wild white violets and foamflowers and the soft green moss Kate sometimes gathered to fill hanging baskets.

Mr. Renty would do well to pick it as a campsite, thought Kate, except that others might think of it and maybe follow him as quickly as she and the Gandy sisters had. The little sand border to the spring had been trampled, but no tracks remained. Kate and the girls stood looking around, uncertain where to go next.

Pine needles obliterated the path and there were no tracks to follow.

"You reckon the river?" asked Sheena.

Kate nodded. The little stream from the spring ran inevitably to the river.

"I bet the Big Rock," said Kim Sue.

Kate squeezed her hand. "I bet you're right. Let's go see."

The walk to the river was not easy. The hill was steep and covered with slippery pine needles. Loose rocks threatened to trip them. In the few sunny spots, briars reached for their clothes and poison ivy was an ever-present menace. They would have welcomed a path, but lacking one they zigzagged between the young pine saplings, grasping them for support when they risked losing their footing. Kate would reach for a tree trunk and swing Kim

Sue along beside her. Sheena grabbed whatever was handy—tree trunk or the skirttail of Kate's good linen suit. Once, Sheena stumbled and fell to her hands and knees and stayed there giggling until Kate put a finger over her lips to shush her and reached out a hand to help her up.

The slope leveled out and they stopped at a point scarred by old fires and littered with beer cans. In years past it amounted to what would have been a gentlemen's club, or at least what in some societies was the pool hall or firehouse. For the men in that end of the county—before the subdivisions came and Animal Control had mixed in—it was the spot where they met on a winter evening to listen to their hound dogs run. They would sit around a fire and pass a bottle, listening attentively to the musical baying of Old Beck and Babe somewhere down the hill in the swamps or pine barrens. It had been a long time since Kate had heard the sweet paeon of hound dogs in the night. She supposed that, intimidated by the encroachment of the city, they didn't come here anymore. Still, she knelt and touched the ashes to see if anybody had been there, specifically if a little old man with a mixing bowl on his head had found it a refuge. The ashes were cold and wet.

She dusted her hands and looked at the girls. "What next?"

"We still got the Big Rock," said Kim Sue.

"Right," Kate said without too much hope. "Lead on."

They found a remnant of a path and the girls capered ahead. Once, when Benjy bought Kate a little bay mare for Christmas, she rode her a month or two before they discovered the horse was blind—how could Benjy have known, a city-reared cop?—and the path to Big Rock was well-known to her. Now it was an "untraveled way," but the girls remembered it. Jutting out from the hillside, a great granite boulder overlooked the river far below. On a fair day you could see the mountains in blue scallops away to the north.

They slid the last few feet and rested together on the lichened flank of the stone leviathan. It was still Kate's favorite spot at any season and she mourned the long-gone times when she and Benjy would eat a sandwich on the rock and swim nude in the river below.

The little girls had revived quickly and were busy trying to land rocks in the river, a sinuous silver target only a pitcher from the Braves would be likely to hit, though the kids always tried. Kate looked around for a right-sized stone she could throw. That led her to the spot she knew they had come to see, the underside of the rock, where it made a shelter of sorts. It was there they found traces of Mr. Renty's habitation: blanket bed, still-live coals encircled by small rocks, a smoky coffeepot, and a dozen apple cores, some of them obviously coon-gnawed.

The Gandys, pushing ahead of her, were charmed with the discovery.

"He lives here. I know'd we'd find him!" caroled Kim Sue.

"Well, we ain't found him yet, dum-dum," said Sheena. "He ain't here, is he?"

Kim Sue was only momentarily disconcerted.

"Aw, he'll be back, won't he, Miss Kate? Ain't this the perfect place to hide away?"

"Ah, yes," said Kate. "I always thought I'd like to live here—maybe in a house a little way up the hill with windows that looked out on the river and the mountains."

They agreed to wait awhile, hoping that Mr. Renty would return, and to pass the time, they slipped and slid down the steep bank to the river, where the girls took off their sneakers and waded. Kate, only momentarily reluctant, followed suit. She tucked the tail of her now ruined linen suit in her underpants and followed the girls to the center of the little river where the clear and icy cold water flowed swiftly over the sand-and-pebble bottom. It wasn't a bad way to spend a Monday morning, she thought, but her conscience began to nag. Since she wasn't at work, she at least could be more zealous about finding Mr. Renty.

In the end, she did go to work, after delivering the Gandys to their family in the little tarpaper-covered house down the road and changing into her pink seersucker suit. The Greens were sitting under the maple tree having a beer when she returned to the cabin.

"Hi!" called Edge. "We washed up the breakfast dishes"—theirs, Kate thought—"and made the bed"—again theirs—"and decided to take a break. The garage man called and the news ain't good. He thinks our car ain't worth fixing. Would you believe it?"

"I guess I'd believe it about almost any car," said Kate.

"Aw, the man's a crook," said Bambi.

"I don't think Dip is a crook," Kate said. "He may have made a mistake or thought you might not want to pay as much as it will cost. I'll stop by and see him on my way to town."

Edge followed her to her car. "I hope you don't mind if we stay with you awhile. I called a friend in Beeville, the one where our little boy Shawn is a-staying. He wants to put Shawn on the bus for Atlanta. Him and his wife are fixing to go somewhere. I told him about the car and he promised to pay Shawn's way and send a little money besides."

"That was nice of him," murmured Kate. "When is Shawn coming?"

"Tomorrow, I reckon," said Edge. "He said he'd send him soonest. By the way, did you find the old man?"

Kate shook her head. She decided not to tell anybody except perhaps Miss Willie that they had seen signs of his camping out. She had warned the Gandy girls and after so many experiences with them, including a couple of murder investigations, she believed them when they crossed their young hearts and hoped-to-die if they told.

The litany of things wrong with the Greens' car was so long and melodious, the way Dip sang it out, that Kate wanted to suggest that he memorize it and try for a place in the Baptist church choir.

"You could make it go, couldn't you? For money, couldn't you?" Kate asked Dip.

"Maybe I could and maybe I couldn't, if I had the rest of my life to work on it," Dip said. "The money would be a humongous amount, too. Parts, not even counting my labor. My advice to you is to call a junkyard, one that will pick it up and not charge you."

"Give me a list, Dip," Kate said by way of leave-taking, "and I'll take it up with Mr. and Mrs. Green."

Before he could sing that one out she waved and started her car. She had one more stop to make on her way to her desk at the *Atlanta Searchlight*: the Dairy Queen across the bridge.

The lunch crowd had not assembled yet and Kate had the attention of the glum-looking man behind the cash register and the two teenage counter attendants. The day had warmed up and the cool air felt good, almost as good as the cold river water, Kate reflected. She ordered a cup of coffee and a grilled cheese sandwich. As she waited she remarked to the cash register man, "Charlene not working today?"

"No, ma'am," he said briefly.

The young girl who brought Kate her coffee and sandwich whispered, "Not today or ever again, we hear. She inherited and she's retired."

"Really?" said Kate, smiling her interest.

The young waitress glanced over her shoulder and caught the eye of the cash register man and went back to her post.

Kate took her time with her coffee and sandwich. How and what had Charlene inherited? She decided to stop by the counter and ask. The help might not be able to talk, but she did not have to obey their rules.

"Charlene still living in the old Renty place?" she asked, getting a refill in her coffee cup. "I have some news for her and I thought I'd run by."

"She's got a telephone," the counter man said shortly.

"Oh, good!" said Kate with excessive enthusiasm. "Give me that number!"

Kate took out a pencil and notebook—one from the office with the logo of the *Atlanta Searchlight* on the cover.

"You from the newspaper?" he asked with a show of interest. That's the way it is, Kate thought. The newspaper connection alarmed and turned off some people or it sparked interest and helpfulness in others. Television, on the other hand, was a surefire charmer. *If I could just tell him I'm Monica Kaufman, WSB's popular anchorwoman,* Kate thought with amusement as he poked through some papers in a drawer, *he'd split his britches helping me.* He helped anyway. He gave her a number.

There were no pay telephones on the premises, so she tucked her notebook back into her bag and hurried to her car. She had heard that pay telephones attracted throngs of teenagers, few of whom were customers, and that was why so few fast food places provided them. By taking the new toll road on 400 she would be in the office in thirty minutes and she would call from there.

Mail and phone messages had piled up over the weekend. She had a column to write and several of her coworkers dropped by. A young male reporter, new to the staff, asked her if she had ever heard of a staff member named Frank L. Stanton.

"Oh, have I ever!" she cried, and began to sing, "Sweetest lil feller, everybody knows. Dunno what to call him but he's mighty lak a rose!"

The young reporter winced. "Did he write that?"

"And a lot of other wonderful stuff," said Kate.

"Well, could you just give me the words without the music?"

Kate ducked her head in mock hurt. "Yep, but you'd miss the melody and the meter of a great life."

"Didn't want that much," the kid said. "It's just part of a piece on the state's poet laureates. Now that I know he worked here, I can look him up on documaster."

"Okay," said Kate, grinning. "You can call up the computer files, but you'd miss so much. He died before my time, but I know a lot about him and I have a couple of his books if you want to borrow them."

"If I do . . ." he lifted his hand in farewell and escaped.

Incompetent, Kate said to herself. *Can't stand a little tuneless croaking in the interest of his story. He'll never make it to a Pulitzer.*

She had swiveled her chair around to face her desk and to make some phone calls, especially the one to Charlene, when a pretty red-haired girl named Deborah or Debra or one of those old-fashioned names that had recently achieved overwhelming popularity tapped meekly on the glass cubicle. Kate was fond of this girl.

"Come in, little Katie," she said. She had been calling the girl that since a security guard got them mixed up and sent people to see the young one, thinking she was Katherine Kincaid Mulcay, the aging veteran. He had no idea about their age difference. Kate considered herself old enough to be the girl's mother. And he certainly had not observed the difference in looks. Maybe at one time, Kate thought wistfully, she had looked like this girl—auburn hair, a piquant face, a slim, athletic body. Now . . . she tried not to think of the wrinkles and bulges and hair going gray.

The girl's face was wet with tears. Kate stood to meet her.

"What ails you, honey?" she asked.

"It's Stan," she said. "He's found somebody else. He doesn't love me!"

"Ah," said Kate, putting an arm around her. "Dumb cluck. If he doesn't love you, he's not worth a tear." She handed the girl a paper handkerchief. And pushed a chair toward her.

"Tell me."

"Well, the other night I left work and went with a crowd to Manuel's and he was there . . . with this blonde! I thought it might be somebody he works with, but when I waved and said 'Come join us,' he just shook his head and in a few minutes they left. Together!"

"If he was at Manuel's Tavern," said Kate—it was an old Atlanta gathering place for politicians and the press—"he was not trying to hide. He would know everybody would see them."

"He did know it," the girl said. "That was what he was doing, showing her off. She works for television and she looks just like . . ." her voice broke and the indictment came out in a rush, "a Barbie doll!"

Kate couldn't help smiling. "Nobody over eight loves Barbie dolls!" she said. "They might play with them, but they're not . . . cuddly."

"I'm not cuddly anymore," wailed Debbie. "He told me that night. He came to my apartment and got his things and left!"

Kate had no solutions. Unless it was something she could call the police or a social worker about or look up at the library, it was a problem beyond her control.

"Ah, honey," she murmured. It was so pitiful to be young and in love, unalloyed vulnerability.

The girl wiped her eyes, blew her nose, and stood up, brushing her mane of shining hair out of her eyes. "I got to go. I'm on obits this week. Could we have lunch one day or maybe . . ." she faltered and grinned the satire, "a beer at Manuel's?"

"Sure," said Kate, standing up. "Let me know."

"Back to my dead people," the girl said. "Wish I was one of them."

"I know," said Kate. "Just put 'em away nice."

She turned to the phone with Charlene's number. A sulky voice answered.

"Charlene?" said Kate with false friendliness. She didn't remember having ever met the woman. "This is Kate—Kate Mulcay. You home all afternoon? I thought I'd stop by."

Clearly astonished, the woman mumbled, "You want to come here?"

"Yes," Kate said. "I really want to see Mr. Renty." And then, inspired, "I have a little gift for him."

"A what?" asked Charlene.

"Oh, a little something," Kate said lightly. "Is he at home?"

"No, no, he ain't," Charlene answered. "I been a-looking for him. But . . ." she rallied, "you could leave it here."

"Fine," said Kate. "I'll do that. Let's see if I remember. You turn off Banks Road, don't you?"

"Yeah, Banks Road to the old sawmill. You go past the sawdust pile and turn left."

"Good. I'll find you," said Kate cheerfully, and hung up the phone before Charlene could change her mind. Now for the gift for Mr. Renty, she thought.

What on earth could she take the old man? Except for blueberries, she had never given him anything in his life. Now . . . she looked around her little office. It was a hodgepodge of stuff. Mostly her own pictures and certificates and muddy loafers she had left under her desk on the last rainy day. Her eye fell on a slim cardboard gift box. A Braves tie, the very thing! Somebody had brought it to her, a wide silk sheath emblazoned with the red-and-white-uniformed figures of the intrepid Atlanta Braves in action. She was a Braves fan, of sorts, but she doubted Mr. Renty had ever heard of them. Nevertheless, it was a fine gift.

She tucked it under her arm, grabbed her bag, and waved at Shell Shelnutt, the city editor.

"Off to a county emergency," she said by way of explanation. Not that Shell cared what hours she kept, as long as she was available when he needed her.

He caught her at the elevator. "I bet I know what the emergency is. Kinfolks visiting from Texas! They stopped by here yesterday." Kate grinned and waved. It was part of the county crisis. She had almost forgotten that she couldn't go home to her log cabin in peace and tranquillity. *They* would be there.

"Thanks for sending them along," she said with false gratitude as the door slid shut.

She loved Atlanta in the late afternoon. A freight train lifted its lonesome halloo up toward Inman Yards—one of the few of the big herd of iron horses that once thundered through Atlanta, making it a railroad center. A helicopter, stabled on top of an office building near the capitol, took to the air and wheeled toward Hartsfield Airport. She yearned after it. She had always wanted a helicopter. They made her laugh, clumsily moving, clucking like an old game rooster. She had a dream of tethering one to her back steps for fast transportation when she needed it.

The policeman at the corner stopped both a Brink's

truck from the Federal Reserve bank and a carload of black teenagers with their radio blasting to let Kate cross the street.

"Thanks, Lieutenant," Kate said, unable to remember his name but recognizing his rank.

"Wait up, Kate," he said, pulling off one of his white gloves. "Got something to tell you. You know that book on Gettysburg that you wrote about?"

Kate nodded, suddenly remembering him. He was a Civil War buff—not one to join in the reenactment of battles, the popular diversion now; he just read all the books and was interested in checking the life of his ancestors who had fought in the Battle of Atlanta.

"What about it?"

"I can't get it," he said. "Out at the library and all the bookstores."

"You can have my copy," said Kate. "I'm through with it. When you have finished snarling up the traffic here, run upstairs and look on my desk. I think it's on top of the pile of stuff."

It was an old joke about snarling traffic. Her father and other old-timers on the force always kidded the rookies that if they would just leave traffic alone and go get a Coke and rest in the shade, it would unsnarl itself.

The officer grinned at her, put his gloves back on, lifted his hand in salute, and blew his whistle to get some big paper truck rolling again. "Thanks," he called. "Buy you a cup of coffee, if you can wait."

"Can't. Sorry," Kate called to him. "Got to go to north Fulton and solve a few crimes." She knew he recognized it as a joke, but she wasn't sure. She had a bad feeling about Mr. Renty. Where was he?

* * *

The old Renty house was easy to find after crossing the river bridge and seeing the Banks Road sign. It had once been a substantial farmhouse in an earlier day, white-painted with a picket fence to separate it from the rutted dirt road. Now time and weather had washed its paint to a skim-milk pallor. One of its porches sagged, taking its roof down with it like a hat over a beggar's eyes. The yard must have been hard-swept in its day. Now it was hard-packed with patches of weeds here and there, and two magnificent magnolia trees blooming on either side of the walk. The picket fence, despite its snaggletoothed look, was supported and ornamented by the darnedest collection of stuffed animals Kate had ever seen. Teddy bears and whales and rabbits and kangaroos leaned against the fence. Kate had the feeling that they were all grinning glassily at her. She paused to count them—a total of ten! She started up the walk past the gate, ajar and hanging by one hinge, when her eyes fell on a man-sized bear by the front door. He was at least six feet tall and he held a violin clasped in one paw against his shoulder and a bow in the other paw, poised over the violin in playing posture.

Suddenly it started sawing the strings and the scratchy tune of "Turkey in the Straw" poured out into the summer air.

"Good Lord!" she whispered, and stopped stock-still.

A giggle sounded behind the half-open front door, "Turkey in the Straw" faltered and scratched to a stop, and a chubby little woman with improbable blue-black hair teased into a tepee and wearing a purple bikini holding an overflow of white thighs together appeared on the porch.

"Got to you, didn't it?" she said. "Most folks are ready to run when they see an artificial bear playing music."

"It was a shock," Kate admitted. "Are you sure he's not a real bear? Or a man in a bear hide?"

"Aw-w!" scoffed the woman. "Stuffed like my little creeturs out by the fence. Uncle Eli done it and then rigged up the fiddle and the music-playing. It's a record. He's electric. Push a button and there he goes!" She pushed a button somewhere beside the bear's ear and the fiddle hit "Dixie."

"We-ell!" gasped Kate, sitting down on the top step. "That's really something!"

The woman let the bear play a full chorus of "Dixie" before she turned him off. Then she came and sat on the step beside Kate.

"You Miz Mulcay, ain't you? I'm Charlene—call me Charlie. You come to bring Uncle Eli something?"

"Yes, I did," said Kate. "Is he at home?"

"No," said Charlene, sighing. "Gone again. He traipses the countryside, Uncle Eli does. But he's been gone longer this time than usual. Left one night last week. I fergit when." She sighed heavily again. "I got to do something about that old feller. He needs to be put away."

"You mean in an institution?" asked Kate.

"I'd say the crazy house," said Charlene, giggling again.

"Oh, I wouldn't do that," murmured Kate. "He is a nice jolly old gentleman and he doesn't do a bit of harm."

"Picks everybody's berries and fruit," said Charlene severely.

"Oh, well," said Kate, "nobody minds that. There's

usually enough to spare. He's welcome to anything on my place."

"You said you was bringing him a present," reminded Charlene.

"Oh, yes," said Kate, standing up. "It's a necktie. I have it in the car. I'll just give it to him when I see him."

"A necktie!" whooped Charlene. "Uncle Eli in a necktie! Good Godamighty, jes' right for Milledgeville!"

"I hope you'll reconsider about Milledgeville," said Kate, thinking of the big state mental hospital where doors were locked and windows were barred and screams of the mad rang out in the night. She had been there many times on stories for the paper and approved of much of the treatment she saw. But Mr. Renty, a merry little man, should be allowed to dance his way through the wooded hills and gardens and orchards of his native north Fulton.

"I got my own ideas," said Charlene stubbornly, following her down to the gate. "I reckon I'm his next of kin and I got the say. By the way," she interrupted herself, "you want to buy some of these creeturs? I usually sell them out by the paved road, but since you come to the house I'll give you the bargain rate."

Over my dead body, Kate said to herself. But she paused. It wouldn't hurt to ingratiate herself with the fool woman if she had the chance to help Mr. Renty. She looked over the stock and left clutching two purple teddy bears under her arms. It was an affront to the teddy bear image, this purple nylon. No teddy bear ought to be purple. Everybody knows that teddy bears are brown. And the wide plastic eyes were an extra insult to all beardom. But the Gandy sisters would like them and maybe if she mollified Charlene she would have second thoughts about committing Mr. Renty.

Charlene tucked Kate's bills in the sweaty chasm between her breasts. Kate got into her car and turned—on another tack.

"This is a sweet old house. Big family house. Do you live here by yourselves, you and Mr. Renty?"

Charlene dimpled copiously. "I got a boyfriend," she confessed. Her face clouded momentarily. "Only trouble is Uncle Eli drives him crazy dancing and capering around like a little young 'un."

"Hmn," sniffed Kate. "That's hard on you, caught in the middle like that. I wouldn't care for a man who didn't like my blood kin."

"Oh, he's mighty cute," said Charlene. "And he is a man. You know how some of us gits—a-wanting a man."

"We-ell," Kate said noncommittally.

"You been a widder woman a long time," pronounced Charlene. "Dried up." She waved and straightened a magenta lamb by the gate.

Kate headed for the paved road thinking, *Am I dried up? Does it happen that you get old and don't long for a man in your life?* She missed her husband acutely, but she liked all men.

She liked the looks of men—the shape of a masculine face, bigger, stronger hands, the sound of a masculine voice. But she hadn't been tempted to covet a man of her own since Benjy died. In fact, she had noticed that men no longer looked at her—not flirtatiously or calculatingly or even with the vaguest passing interest. They simply looked somewhere else when they passed on the street or shared an elevator or stood near her to wait for a traffic light. She understood, but she couldn't help feeling bereft now and then.

Edge and Bambi were in the yard when she drove in, waiting for her to provide their supper, she supposed.

"Sorry to be late," she said when they walked out to meet her. "You all starving?"

"You don't know my Bambi if you think that," said Edge. And for a fleeting moment Kate thought that Bambi had managed to scare up a meal. He straightened that out immediately.

"Some of the neighbors across the road saw her out walking and invited us to come over for a barbecue. And bring you, of course."

"How nice," murmured Kate. "Which house? You remember their names?"

"Bets and Bobby," said Bambi. "It's the flesh-colored stucco."

"That's the Dunns," she said, "and it's very nice of them. You all go ahead and thank them for me and tell them I'll get there as soon as I can. I've got one pretty important assignment to finish first."

They seemed glad enough to go without her and Kate watched them cross the road. Suddenly she realized that they were visible for a longer time than was usual. She walked toward the thicket which concealed her yard from the road. Only the thicket wasn't there anymore!

In the falling darkness it was perfectly apparent that half the trees and bushes she had so lovingly planted to screen off the road had been whacked down.

"Edge!" she called after him. "Edge! What happened here? Where is my thicket?"

He turned back and came toward her, grinning fatuously.

"Thought you'd be surprised," he said. "Took me most of the day, but Bobby lent me his chain saw. I knew you'd like it. He said it would give you a clear view of the subdivision—and them of you."

"Oh, dear God!" cried Kate, and burst into tears.

Bambi had walked on and Edge apparently thought Kate was indulging in a paroxysm of joy.

"Thought you'd like it, Cuz," he said, and Kate realized he was waiting for her thanks.

"It's . . . it's something," she finally gasped.

"Yeah," he said. "Bambi thought she saw a snake in there and that's what got me started."

"I wish . . ." Kate had started to storm *I wish it had bitten her.* But she regained control and said nothing. She had spent twenty years assembling that thicket, starting with the young pine trees and one old crape myrtle bush that was there when she and Benjy had arrived. Gradually they had added hollies and hemlocks, one sweet bay tree, and a couple of swamp myrtles. Every time she saw an interesting shrub at the garden center she would buy it and find a spot for it. There were two big viburnums that were her pride and joy, one Chinese dogwood, and one young flowering crabapple she and the Gandy sisters had planted in the spring. It had been her aim to make the thicket impenetrable and it pleased her when people said, "I saw the roof of your log cabin when I passed there, but you got a real green wall between you and the road. I couldn't see anything else."

Fine, thought Kate. *Now it's picked as bare as a Thanksgiving turkey,* she reflected bitterly. She walked out in the road to see the complete horror of it and Edge walked on after Bambi.

It's not my house anymore, she thought despairingly. *I'll have to give it to them.*

She turned her back on the wasteland and walked toward the back door. What had she been planning to do? Somehow nothing seemed worth her doing, she thought despondently. Then she remembered Mr. Renty. She meant to take him food and a sleeping bag.

She'd never tell that stuffed-animal fool, Charlene or Charlie, where he was, *if* he was still camping out under the Big Rock. But she was afraid he was hungry, and although the weather was warm, he would probably get chilly toward morning or attacked by mosquitoes. She went upstairs and pulled Benjy's old sleeping bag out of a box under the bed. The larder yielded but little—some bread and eggs, a piece of cheese, and some fruit. She found some matches for his fire-building and a flashlight to help her find the way once she had passed the carnage of her yard, and began her journey through the woods. She took her car as far as Mr. Banana Pierce's old house site and hid it behind the trifoliata bush so that the Dunns, in case they or any of their other guests came that way, would not know that her "assignment" was in the area.

The walk to the Big Rock was even trickier than it had been in the morning, and Kate, remembering Bambi's reported snake, kept flashing her light from side to side peering into the bushes. Once a hoot owl sounded in the woods and before she recognized its origin, she stopped dead still, fighting the impulse to turn and run. She wasn't scared of hoot owls in the middle of the night—but they did send cold shivers up her spine, she admitted. It might be, as the bird books said, a questing love call, but in the woods in the dark of night it sounded like a call from the dead.

She was relieved to arrive at her first landmark, the old cold fire of the fox hunters. After that it was literally downhill and she was relieved. Even the down-filled sleeping bag had grown heavy, and her little plastic sack of food threatened to split and spill.

When she finally saw the hulking silhouette of the Big Rock, she rotated her light and called out softly, "Mr. Renty, you here? It's Kate Mulcay, I've come to see you."

There was no answer and when she finally slid down the bank to where she could see under the rock, there was nobody there. There were still live coals in the little circle of rocks and steaming water in the old coffeepot.

Kate eased her burden down and flashed her light down the hill and over the top of the rock.

"Mr. Renty," she pleaded. "Come on out. It's just me, Kate. I've got you something to eat."

There was no answer.

She found a chunk of oak and put it on the fire. In a moment it caught and blazed up, casting fingers of golden light on the sides and overhang of the rock.

"Well, I'm gon' wait," she finally said, apparently to nobody at all. "I'm scared to stay out here all by myself, but you're my friend, Mr. Renty, and I'll wait."

There was no sign of movement anywhere and Kate wondered if the old man had gone down to the river to get water. Or . . . a frightening idea took hold. Was he nowhere here? Was he dead? Was she trespassing on some bum's campsite? Did she have reason to be, as she had proclaimed, scared?

She tried once more without much hope. "I brought you a necktie!"

Suddenly the little man was there. He moved silently almost as airborne as a ghost, but he had her yellow bowl full of water in his hands and he set it down gently.

"Where?" he asked suddenly. "Where's my necktie?"

Kate started laughing.

"It's here somewhere," she said, rummaging in her plastic bag. "Food, too. But Mr. Renty . . ." she suddenly saw his face and arms. "You're hurt. You been bleeding and you're all bruised."

He wasn't listening. His eyes were on the slim box Kate was bringing out of her bag.

"Necktie," he whispered, and grabbed it away from her. While she watched, he brought it around his scrawny, bruised old neck with its spots of dried blood and tied it in front with a neat four-in-hand.

He lifted his old legs as if to do a jig, but they apparently hurt him too much and he simply sat down, caressing the tie with scarred, dried, blood-streaked hands.

"Mr. Renty, I'm gon' take you to a doctor," Kate said in sudden decision. "I think you're worse hurt than I realized. What were you beaten with?"

The old gentleman caressed his necktie dreamily and said nothing.

Kate stood up. "Come on. We're going to get those cuts and bruises cleaned up and take you to the doctor."

He shook his dandelion head and smoothed the agile Braves at play down on his dirty shirt.

"No, no, no, no!" he sang, and made a poor imitation of an effort to skip down the bank toward the river. "They'll git the battling stick."

"The what?" said Kate. And then she knew. Not a military weapon as she had first supposed, but a stout lye-bleached oak stick used by country women in the pre-Maytag days to whack the dirt out of wet clothes.

"Did they hit you with a battling stick?" she demanded.

The old man flipped up his ragged shirttail as he hobbled down the bank, exposing in the flickering firelight raw cuts and bruises across his scrawny back.

"Dear God," whispered Kate, sitting down again. "You're hurt bad, Mr. Renty. We got to go."

But the old man had vanished into the dark woods.

Kate knew she was going to cry out of helpless horror. "Please come back," she begged tearfully. "Come back, Mr. Renty!"

But the old man did not come back. The chunk of oak wood burned low and Kate sat on, using her skirt tail in the absence of a handkerchief to mop at the tears which flowed down her cheeks. She didn't know whether she was crying for Mr. Renty, a helpless old man, or for herself and her brutalized yard.

Hours later—Kate didn't know how long she had sat waiting for Mr. Renty to return—she drove into her driveway and found that the old farm lantern in the persimmon tree had been replaced in her absence with a floodlight. Inside, the house was dark and she assumed that Edge and Bambi had gone to bed. As she reached the steps, she heard Bambi giggle and she stopped.

I can't go in there, she said to herself. *I can't. I've had enough today.* She sat down on the steps and looked at the merciless light they had poured over her little country yard, robbing it of its charm and its mystery. *They'll pave it next,* she thought. *Tomorrow I'll ask them to leave.*

Kate couldn't bear to go in the house. She looked beyond her decimated thicket toward Miss Willie's old house on the river. She had spent the night with Miss Willie a few times in the past when she had been ill and the old woman determined that she needed to be "sick nussed." Miss Willie had stayed with her when her own house had been taken from her by a stepson who eventually was found dead there. They were, as Miss Willie said, strengthening to one another.

Kate found a scrap of paper in her bag and wrote a note. She didn't want Edge and Bambi getting alarmed and calling out the police. She tucked it in the screen door, gave Pepper a pat and a whispered invitation to join her. The dog frisked ahead and she followed wearily across the road and through the subdivision.

Waking up at Miss Willie's was comforting. The night before, the old woman had started to lead her to her spare room, but one look at Kate's face and torn stocking, her stained and torn suit in the gentle light of the kerosene lamp changed her mind.

"You git in bed with me," she said, handing Kate a clothesline-fragrant nightgown made years ago out of feed sacks boiled and sunbleached to whiteness. "You need warmth."

Miss Willie may have meant she needed the little summer quilt she spread over her, but Kate knew the important warmth was from the old bony arm that she put around her and the rough old hand that held one of hers. She went to sleep feeling loved and looked after.

Miss Willie was up early with her big gray granite coffeepot with its drip bag full of hand-ground coffee sending out a heavenly fragrance. She was rolling and pinching off hefty-sized biscuits when Kate tottered, heavy-eyed, into the kitchen. When she had had one cup of coffee and one biscuit, she told Miss Willie about the day before's vicissitudes—first Charlene's admission that she wanted to put Mr. Renty away in a mental institution. And then about Mr. Renty's physical state when she tracked him down at his little camp spot. As an afterthought and after two more cups of coffee and another biscuit, Kate told her about the atrocities committed in her yard.

Miss Willie pulled up her little kitchen rocker and poured herself another cup of coffee.

"Tell me about them people," she said. "Air they well-kin to Benjamin?"

"I don't know!" Kate cried. "I haven't any idea. The man says they're cousins. They had the same grandmother. But I don't know."

"Not well-kin," said Miss Willie judiciously. "You'll be justified showing them the road."

"I'm going to," said Kate resolutely. "I am going straight home and throw 'em out!"

"Where will they go?" asked Miss Willie hesitantly, as if it were a question best not raised. Kate gulped and looked out across the yard.

"That's the trouble. Their car won't run. I don't think they have a dime. He lost his job and their house in Texas! Oh, Miss Willie!"

Miss Willie nodded understandingly. "You'll do the right thing, Kate, and that'll mean putting up with them a spell until their luck changes."

Kate sighed with resignation. But when she got back to her own yard, she found Edge going around the porch with a pruning saw in hand.

"Wait, wait!" she cried. "Where are you going with that saw?"

He smiled indulgently. "Just thought I'd tackle this dead old peach tree."

"*No!*" shouted Kate. "That peach tree's only half dead. It was here when we came. I know it's decaying at the base, but see that vine?"

"Honeysuckle," pronounced Bambi from the back steps.

"It is not!" Kate shouted with unwonted fury. "It's a silver lace vine and it's just about to bloom! The peach tree supports it."

"Oh," said Edge, dismayed.

"Hmn," sniffed Bambi contemptuously.

"And another thing . . ." began Kate. But she couldn't go on. They had to go, but she couldn't put them out until they had a plan. "I think your car is hopeless."

Edge nodded soberly, but then he rallied. "We got a call late last night from Beesville. Our friends put our boy Shawn on the Greyhound. Paid his fare. Due in at six P.M. today. Reckon you could meet him, seeing as we are out of a car?"

On the way to town, Kate shifted the problem of the Greens to give precedence to the problem of Mr. Renty. Her instinct was to go to the police with the story of his beating. But he would refuse to testify, for fear of that battling stick, and even if she enlisted the police to help her get him to a doctor, he would probably run or find a new hiding place. The best she could do, at least temporarily, was take him more food and some remedies for his wounds. She would like to do that early in the evening to make the trip to the Big Rock easier, but if she had to claim Shawn at the bus station it would be at least seven o'clock before she got home.

She sighed and went into the office hoping for something cheerful—a mass murder, a political scandal, maybe even a big fire—just something to take her mind off the piddling cares that seemed to beset her.

Instead, it was another kind of besetting day. Calls and mail asking her to do things she had no taste for—to be somewhere, give something, publicize, contribute, speak, expose. She had always worried over letters from prisoners, to the point of writing persuasively enough for some of them to get paroled and find jobs and places to live, only—in the most recent instances—to have them steal from the people her prose had persuaded to help them, and then to disappear.

That day her problem was nice little high school students who proposed that she write their themes for them. They weren't that open about it.

A typical letter read: "Dear Miss Kincaid, You are my favorite southern writer. Will you answer these questions for me, please?" There followed a page of eight or ten multiple-answer questions about her life, achievements, philosophy, and remedies for world crisis and environmental decay. It ended: "Please answer as soon as possible. I have to have it for English lit. Type. Double space.

Your friend, Jennifer." (No last name and an unclear return address.)

By five o'clock Kate was glad to turn off her computer and quit her office. She didn't mind waiting for Shawn in the bus station. In the war years she had developed an affection for this place of arrival and departure, but the station, airport, and railroad depot seemed to have grown stale. Exhausted young mothers chased little children, old ladies clutched their pocketbooks and checked their tickets again and again. A drunk saw a policeman coming and wove swiftly but uncertainly to the men's room. Kate hoped he got in and locked himself in a cubicle before the law caught up with him. She saw no sweet partings between young couples. There were some soldiers catching a bus for Fort McPherson out on the edge of town, but nobody was there to see them off. *Be glad it's peacetime,* Kate admonished herself, adding, *Besides, it's a suburban bus.*

She smelled hamburgers offered by the bus station lunchroom, old coffee, box lunches with bananas and hard-boiled eggs, unwashed bodies, and the soapy water and disinfectant a porter was sloshing over the tiled floor with a mop. The loudspeaker blared out destinations and arrivals, and she liked them all, especially the ones that promised a trip to small towns, although the sound of faraway places—New York, Boston, Chicago—was enticing. She had lost track of the time when the loudspeaker hailed a Scenicliner from Texas. That would be Shawn, she decided.

She walked to the door and watched a crowd of tired, gray-faced people stumble off. Finally there was a child, dragging a canvas duffle bag behind him. He had a shock of tow hair and a small pinched face that bore the streaks and strains of a day on the bus and rest stop candy bars and egg salad sandwiches. His blue jeans were dingy and too tight—overgrown tight, not fashion tight, Kate decided. He wore an Astros T-shirt. He looked around anxiously and stopped in the middle of the stream of alighting passengers.

"Get on out of the way, kid," a man back of him growled. The boy looked over his shoulder nervously and tugged at his duffle bag.

"Shawn!" called Kate, going to the rescue. "Here! Come on over here. You made it!" she added. She pushed forward and reached to give him a hand with his duffle bag. He let it go but searched her face suspiciously.

"I'm your cousin Kate." Suddenly she felt glad to accept the relationship.

"Where's my mama and my daddy?" he asked.

Of course, in this day of kidnappers and child molesters they had been stupid to send her, a stranger, to get him and she was stupid to have accepted the assignment.

"They couldn't come because their car broke down," she said. "They sent me. We'll go call them. They are so glad you're coming and they'll want to talk to you right away!"

She led the way to a pay phone in the station and dialed her house. Bambi answered.

"I've got somebody here who wants to talk to you," she said, handing the phone to Shawn.

He clutched the phone in a dirty hand like it was a lifeline. His voice was low and timid. Kate heard noises from Bambi and then from Edge and saw the young face clear and the dark gray eyes light up.

"Tell them we're on our way," Kate prompted. And then as an afterthought, "Tell them we'll bring pizza for supper."

Except for checking out the make and year of Kate's car, Shawn had little to say on the trip to the cabin. Kate strove for conversation but finally gave up and concentrated on the traffic and a new worry: Where would they put this newest newcomer to sleep?

Shawn's pleasure in a log cabin and the prospect of pizza for supper was very disarming. He came to life as the headlights picked up the log walls.

"Hey, it looks like Fort Apache!" he cried, sitting up straight. "Is it an Indian fort?"

"No, but it's sort of pioneerish," said Kate. "It's been here a long time." Her hope was that it was still all there, that the Greens hadn't decided to demolish it like the thicket.

But they were glad to see their child, Kate admitted, and she gave them points for that. They came out to the driveway to meet him and to carry in the pizza and his duffle bag. They hugged him, and Bambi held his hand as they walked toward the house.

"Is this where we're staying?" the little boy asked, looking around. "Neato."

Bless your heart, Kate thought, her eyes resting on the narrow young body, the pinched little face. *No telling how much you have been pushed around.* She realized then that she couldn't evict the Greens yet, not for a while.

Poor baby, she thought, in the words of the old spiritual, *this world is not his home. Not yet.* She found herself wanting to make him feel at home.

* * *

Miss Willie was glad to see Kate as she came up to her house. She had been assembling some food to take to Mr. Renty herself but she had had a notion to wait for Kate.

"I'm glad you came," she said. "Two hands is better than one."

Kate stuffed in her pack a jar of hot beans Miss Willie had picked out of her garden that morning and cooked, well seasoned with salt bacon. She had a cake of cornbread in a small iron skillet, which she planned to leave with Mr. Renty for use on his campfire.

Kate worried that the rough woods trip in the darkness might be too much for Miss Willie and then she smiled at her effrontery. The woods, day or night, rough or smooth, were Miss Willie's natural habitat. Eighty-odd years had done little to diminish the old lady's vigor. Grief over the death of her stepson and his aborted effort to put her in a nursing home and take her old house and the last of her land from her had drained her strength and the will to live. But when that was settled, and his wife and fellow drug dealers had been removed from the Shine Creek settlement, Miss Willie had rallied. Now, looking at her in the light of one of her old kerosene lamps which Miss Willie used to avoid the cost and rude brightness of "the electric," Kate saw only energy and vitality in the lean old body and the furrowed old face under its tight bun of gray hair.

With Pepper leading the way, they took off down a narrow path along Miss Willie's little creek. It was a path Kate had not traveled and she noted without surprise that it was easier walking and apparently a little shorter than the route she had been taking.

"This leads to the old whiskey still, doesn't it?" she whispered to Miss Willie.

"Did," said Miss Willie, chuckling. "'Twarn't wise, neither. Them revenuers could foller a clare path as well as the next one."

It was as close as Miss Willie came to admitting she and her late husband had supplemented the poor income of their farm with the manufacture of white whiskey.

When the creek broadened and flowed into the river, Miss Willie paused and looked around her. Suddenly she clambered over a big rock that seemed to guard the way to an arrangement of smaller rocks scattered over the hillside like chairs in a waiting room.

"Miss Willie," Kate whispered. "I haven't seen this place before. What is it?"

"We call it 'Rock Church,'" said the old woman. "Me and Cy rested here many a day after hard work. Smooth rocks for cheers. I thought Mr. Renty might be a-using it."

"His fire and bed are under the Big Rock," Kate said.

"It's a climb to go there," Miss Willie said. "Come on!"

Miss Willie hitched up her old gray skirt and struck out up the hill in the darkness. Pepper, catching her direction, ran ahead. Kate stumbled after.

They had walked for only a few minutes when Pepper barked, his intruder and then his friend-approaching bark.

"He's here," said Miss Willie.

The old man was indeed there. By the light of Kate's flashlight, they found him stretched out on the sleeping bag Kate had brought, shivering and coughing.

"Lord God, he's sick," said Miss Willie, kneeling down and putting her palm on his forehead. "Fever," she said.

Miss Willie looked at the dirt-crusted cuts and bruises

on his arms and gently turned the little body a bit and lifted his shirt so she could see his back.

"I don't care what he says," said Kate, distressed. "We've got to get help and get him out of here!"

Miss Willie sat back on her heels and studied the poor crumpled little man with his nimbus of white hair.

His lips were moving and he was whispering something. Kate leaned closer. It was the refrain of earlier in the day: "No, no, no!"

"Mr. Renty," she began firmly, "you need to be in the hospital or at least where a doctor can see you."

"Battling stick," he whispered.

She looked at Miss Willie in anguish. "That's what they beat him with."

"Lord God," whispered Miss Willie. "Like dirty drawers. They ought to be kilt."

Kate poured hot water out of the thermos into her yellow bowl and began swabbing the cuts with a soapy washcloth. Miss Willie spread out the bottles and tubes she had brought.

"These will help mollify his cuts," she said, "until daylight when I can git Queen of the Meader. He needs that."

"Miss Willie," Kate said gently, "your herb medicines will help him, I know. But don't you think we'd best get him to a doctor?"

"If we could," said Miss Willie. "But you and me together can't tote him through the woods at night and he ain't strong enough for it." She grinned. "Even if we was to be. Tomorrow . . . I don't know, honey. Maybe the law?"

"Definitely the law," said Kate, who had unshakable

belief in the powers of the police. They would know what to do with a gurney and an ambulance with a Grady Hospital intern in attendance if they were lucky. Her belief in old Grady Hospital was second only to her faith in the efficacy of calling the police.

In the meantime, they would do what they could. They bathed and bandaged him, working around the ridiculous necktie until the old man moaned in pain. Kate took his shoes off his swollen feet and used the last of the warm water to wash them.

"He needs clean clothes," said Miss Willie. She fingered her voluminous old skirt thoughtfully.

"No, you don't," said Kate. "Let's put my jeans on him. Too big, but they won't embarrass him when help comes."

Miss Willie didn't mention that walking through the woods in her underpants, Kate's legs would be cut into ribbons by briars. She knew it was the only practical thing to do. The night was getting chilly for summertime. His shirt was not only filthy, but it offered no warmth. Miss Willie was equal to the problem. She pulled off her shirtwaist and eased his scrawny arms into the long sleeves.

Kate couldn't help grinning. She had never seen Miss Willie so close to unclad, but the old lady handled it with her usual resourcefulness. She took off her generously cut gingham apron and draped it over her shoulders, tying the strings beneath her chin.

"Now!" she said. "Let's see if we can git some vittles in him."

Surprisingly, the old man seemed a little stronger. He nodded when they offered him food, and while Miss

Willie heated the beans and cornbread on the remaining coals in the little campfire, Kate lifted him and got a swallow or two of orange juice down him.

When they could think of nothing else to do, they put a chunk of wood on the fire and stood up to go.

"I'm a-thanking you," the old man whispered.

"We'll see you in the morning," Kate said.

"Nobody else," he said. "Don't bring nobody else."

Kate wasn't going to make any promises. Miss Willie handled it. "We'll see how you do. I think Queen of the Meader will take care of your fever."

It wasn't a promise, but it was hope and the old man sighed and closed his eyes.

When they were out of earshot, Kate said, "I'm scared, Miss Willie. He could die, couldn't he?"

"He could," said Miss Willie. "If there's infection—blood poisoning."

The Greens were quiet and apparently asleep when Kate returned to the cabin. Shawn was scrunched up on the borrowed rollaway bed in a fetal position, in front of the old fireplace, his bare feet looking big for his skinny legs, his tow head tucked into his thin chest. Chilly herself from the walk through the woods in her underpants, Kate pulled a time-shirred quilt out of the blanket chest in the corner and spread it over him. A blanket felt good to her when she had sponged off the scratches on her legs at the kitchen sink and opened up the sofa bed and lay down.

She wondered if she should call out emergency crews tonight or if she dared wait until morning. While she pondered the question, she slipped into sleep and did not awaken until the sun was up and Miss Willie was calling from the back door. Kate had overslept.

She stumbled out of bed and greeted the old lady with a grin. "Good to see you with your clothes on, Miss Willie."

"Pshaw, you wasn't so modest yourself," said the old woman. "He's gone, Kate. Mr. Renty's gone."

"How do you know, Miss Willie?"

"Well, I had a supply of Queen of the Meader and I made up a tea and fixed some poultices and went up there at first light."

"Without me?" said Kate, aggrieved.

"Didn't make no difference," said Miss Willie. "He was gone. I waited in case he had gone to the bushes to excuse hisself or to the river for water. He never come."

Kate sat down hard on the back step.

"You think he felt that much better?"

"That," said Miss Willie, "or he was scared. Or when an animal . . . Well, no, he ain't no animal."

Kate knew what she had started to say. Animals about to die seek hiding, often a spot by the water.

"I'm gon' call the Fulton County police!" Kate said, standing up.

Shawn wandered out to the porch, his eyes wide. "Police?" he whispered.

"Friends of mine," Kate said quickly. No child should be afraid of the police. "I'm calling to ask them for help."

"Oh, Cuz'n Kate," he pleaded, "don't do that! Please, ma'am, don't do that!"

Kate turned to him.

"Why, Shawn? Do you know something bad about the police?"

Before he could answer, Bambi called from the living

room, "Come here, Shawn! Right now . . . I mean it!"

Kate and Miss Willie exchanged glances. When Shawn did not return to the back porch, Kate went into the kitchen and found Edge putting on the coffee.

"What's the matter with Shawn and the police?" she asked. "I was going to call them to find old Mr. Renty and he seemed upset."

"Aw, that ain't anything," said Edge. "His mama . . ."

"What about his mama?" demanded Bambi from the living room door. "Don't you say a word about me!"

"Nothing," said Edge. "Call the police if you want to. I'll explain to Shawn."

"You'll explain nothing to Shawn!" shouted Bambi. "Come on, son. Let's get out of here!"

She grabbed the little boy's hand and they walked toward the front yard.

Kate looked questioningly at Edge.

"She's just taking him over to Bets and Bob's. She wants him to see their house. They're kinda new friends for her. It's all right. Here, have a cup of coffee. You, too, Miss Willie?"

The old lady shook her head. "No, much obliged. I've had a pot this morning. I'll go on home, Kate. You'll let me know."

Kate thought it was a little early for Bambi to be calling on neighbors, but she said nothing and turned back to the phone. Friends at the county police promised to send somebody, but there was a delay when Kate mentioned the missing person's name.

"Old Mr. Renty?" said Corky. "Kate, you know that old feller runs away all the time. I'd just as soon look for a wild goat."

When she explained about the beating, probably at the hands of his niece, the officer was more interested.

"We'll go there first. Maybe he went back home. Or maybe she found him and is trying to make it up to him."

Kate sniffed. She didn't think Charlene was likely to be overcome with remorse.

Kate gave Corky detailed directions for finding the old Renty home place, throwing in the names of neighbors who might help if all directions failed. Then she described the little camp spot under the Big Rock in case the old man had returned to it.

"You want to come with us, don't you, Kate?" asked Corky. "You always get a personal stake in these cases."

"Oh, no!" Kate said hastily. She did want to go with them, but there was no use letting her pals at the police department think that she had become a cop shop groupie. After all, she had a job to do.

"But please let me know if you find Mr. Renty," she begged. "And if you get him to Grady Hospital. I think he's in bad shape."

Officer Corcoran agreed to call her and Kate made up her mind to push aside her worries over what she obviously could not help. She showered and rummaged for something to wear to the office. Her weekend had given her no time for washing and pressing or mending or even shopping for something to wear to town. She chose a reliable navy blue skirt and a white blouse, clean and respectable, but nothing spirit-uplifting. *Someday,* she always thought on these mornings, *I'm going to buy some clothes.*

She was leaving when Edge came toward the back steps.

"Would you like me and Bambi to go to the grocery store?" he asked.

"Oh, I certainly would!" cried Kate. "I'm sorry I have been so bogged down in other things I forgot about food. Would you want to take me to the MARTA stop and keep the car?"

His face brightened.

"Bambi and Shawn would like that," he said. "They need to get away. When would you like us to pick you up?"

Kate said she would call from the office when she saw what she had to do and Edge hastily rounded up his wife and son for the ride to the bus stop. They had apparently found Bets and Bob still asleep. Bambi made no comment, but she looked disappointed.

Poor things, Kate thought. *They've felt trapped—and I thought I was the one who was trapped.* She turned the steering wheel over to Edge and emptied her purse for grocery money, handing a $20 and a $10 bill to Bambi.

The ride to town by bus and by train was a parole, a sort of furlough from things she couldn't do anything about, Kate always thought, and today it seemed especially so. She rummaged in her bag for a book to read as she climbed aboard the big MARTA bus, knowing she would have a small one—an inspirational volume that had been her grandmother's. It was called *Daily Strength for Daily Needs* and it had a page of inspiration and direction for every day of the year. She opened it at random. She was not careful to match the offerings of the little book to the calendar, feeling a sort of superstition that what her fingers turned to would be what she needed.

Today it seemed particularly true. The paragraph of

scripture was from Psalms and it began, "Why art thou cast down, O my soul? and why art thou disquieted within me? Hope thou in God."

And what Kate supposed was the homily by Saint Francis de Sales warned, "Beware of letting your care degenerate into anxiety and unrest, tossed as you are amid the winds and waves of sundry troubles."

That's me, thought Kate, *anxiety and unrest, tossed amid winds and waves of sundry troubles.* Did Saint Francis know about the troubles of a little man like Mr. Renty or the worries posed by visiting kin? She read on. "We shall steer safely through every storm, so long as our heart is right, our intention fervent, our courage steadfast, and our trust in God. . . . Do not be disconcerted by the fits of vexation and uneasiness which are sometimes produced by the multiplicity of your domestic worries. No indeed, dearest child, all these are but opportunities of strengthening yourself in the loving, forebearing graces which our Lord sets before us."

Kate closed the little book and looked out the window. The road down 400 was almost a passage through a green tunnel of pines until it reached Sandy Springs and the perimeter highway and its tall office buildings. She should pray, she thought. She usually did.

The toll house loomed and the bus zipped right on past it in the "cruise card" lane which was used by buses only, and the new part of the highway took over—steep banks smoothed and planted with small trees and shrubs, each little sapling supported by a new pine stake. Kate envied the plentitude of young trees and the labor to plant and tend them. She thought of her own hard-won thicket and she knew once more that she had to do something to get the Greens on their way. *Intention fervent, courage steadfast,* she thought—and she had neither. If it weren't for the child, his pleasure in an Apache-like log cabin, his sudden fear of the police . . . How could she do anything to make his life more precarious? It had occurred to her to check her savings at the newspaper credit union. She could draw it out and give it to them. What did she have? Five hundred dollars or maybe more? She had drawn some out to buy a new car a few months before. But whatever she had, it would not be enough to house and feed three people for long, particularly since they had no means of transportation.

The bus swerved to the right, taking the Buckhead ramp, and Kate looked at it with pride. Handsome hotels—the big Ritz-Carlton, malls with all the stylish and expensive stores, restaurants where she never ate anymore but which she was glad to see there. A cosmopolitan city, her Atlanta.

The bus crossed Peachtree Road, passing Lenox Square, the town's first big mall, and turned into Lenox Road, and then into the MARTA train station.

The bus driver said "Have a good day," and Kate looked at him apologetically. When she took the bus, she always read her newspaper on the way into town and offered it to the bus driver when they got to the train station. "Sorry. No news for you today," she said. "Got company at my house. Job hunting. They need the ads."

"My sympathy is with you," said the driver, a smiling, neatly groomed black fellow who always kept his uniform jacket buttoned over a burgeoning belly. "My wife's cousin is at my house."

Kate offered him an understanding grimace and ran to

catch the train, which she heard pulling into the station beneath the platform. The little MARTA trains were fast and regular, coming every six minutes or so from Chamblee and Brookhaven, bringing northside workers downtown and taking passengers to the airport, which Kate considered a major civic feat—a transit system that went right into the terminal just a few steps away from the ticket counters. She was a MARTA booster anyhow, exulting in the cleanliness of buses and trains, the lack of torn upholstery and graffiti that marred the systems she had seen in other cities.

By the time she got to the office she was almost optimistic. Although she had worked there since before the security guards were born, she always stopped at the front desk to let them see that she wore her ID card. It was not an accurate one. In a moment of caprice, she had lied to the young typist who had taken down the information for her card, misspelling her name and making herself a lissome twenty-year-old. The child had obediently typed whatever Kate had dictated and now for five or six years Kate had worn the phony ID card, even braving the Secret Service on a quick stop at the White House. It cheered her, somehow, to see the failure of red tape. Today, Stanley, one of the guards, flagged her to a stop.

"You got a crazy lady waiting for you upstairs."

"She can't be bad crazy or you wouldn't have let her in, would you?"

"Aw, she bribed us!" said one of Stanley's young black junior officers. "She brings cakes."

"I bet that's Armageddon," said Kate. "She always comes bringing one of her cakes."

"Two today," admitted Stanley, grinning.

The woman waiting on the sofa in the hall was slender, with white hair carefully coiffed and makeup skillfully applied. She wore a crisp, pretty shirtmaker dress, pearl earrings, and white sandals. On the sofa beside her sat a big cake box.

Kate went forward to meet her, scouring her memory for her name. The staff had privately called her Armageddon for so long it was difficult to remember that she was Mrs. Somebody or Other. She had come one day to tell Kate that Armageddon was imminent and, needing a column that day, Kate had said, "Why not?" Who knew when Armageddon was coming? This pretty lady with the wonderful cakes might know as much about it as anybody. They had become fast friends. The date when that final battle between good and evil written about in the Book of Revelation would take place had changed from time to time, but the lady was undismayed. Every time she had a new vision, she baked a cake—or two—and came to tell Kate about it.

She stood up to give Kate a hug and Kate said, "Come on in," leading the way to her office. "I'm glad to see you. What's new?"

"Armageddon," said the lady.

Kate carefully refrained from saying, *What, again?* It seemed suitable to receive the news with awe. "Tell me about it," she said, pushing her little Naugahyde and chrome visitor's chair forward and breathing deeply of the sweet chocolate fragrance from the cake box.

"Here," said the lady, smiling comfortably and setting the cake on top of the paper slide on Kate's desk. "Well, I just want to tell you to get ready. The forces are gathering. It's going to be Thursday, the twelfth."

"Oh, my," Kate said helplessly. She had read her Revelation, and the horned beasts and the snakes and creatures with many eyes scared her enough to keep her out of that portion of the Bible. "What can I do? I mean personally. I don't think the editor will let me write about it again."

"Thou art neither hot nor cold," said Armageddon sternly. "Because thou art lukewarm the Lord will spew you out of his mouth!"

"Oh, I'm not lukewarm," protested Kate. "I'm . . ." She didn't know what she was. She didn't think she'd mind anything final, battle or not—just to get on with her life. She wanted to investigate the chocolate cake and make some phone calls.

Armageddon stood up. "I must run," she said. "I have my bridge club this afternoon." She was halfway through the city room before Kate rallied to follow her. "He that hath ears to hear, let him hear!" the woman called gaily, and disappeared toward the elevator.

"Whoo!" said Kate, sighing heavily and returning to her desk. Her colleagues, who had seen Armageddon and the cake box, were arriving. Kate pushed the cake box into the food editor's hands and said, "Get a knife and some paper plates. I'll be out there in a minute."

First she had to call the police about Mr. Renty.

Her friend Corky answered. "Just getting ready to call you, Kate. No sign of anybody at the old homestead and we checked out the woods around there and the old fellow was nowhere to be found."

"Did you check the Big Rock I told you about?"

"Naw, I don't think so," said Corky. "Them boys don't like to go anywhere they can't go in a patrol car. They didn't have no search warrant, but there was some blood on the porch. A little. Could be an animal."

"Mr. Renty's," said Kate grimly. "They beat him, I think his precious niece and her boyfriend. Find 'em, Corky. I'm going to look for the old man. If he's not dead. He had fever last night."

"He did? Well, Kate, wait a minute. I'll send—"

"Never mind," said Kate, and hung up the phone.

She paused long enough to tell Shell, the city editor, she was leaving. But between some computer copy he had on his screen and a big wedge of chocolate cake he had in his hand, he didn't pay much attention.

Kate got a staff car and went as straight as she could to the Big Rock, parking the unmarked car across the river, at the nearest access spot. She took off her shoes and panty hose and jumped from rock to rock where possible, and waded the rest of the way. Her skirt tail was wet but the midday sun warmed her, and when she reached the shore she put her shoes back on, stuffing her panty hose in her pocket.

The climb to the rock seemed steeper than she remembered, but she made it pretty fast. She had barely scrambled up the last steep bank when she saw the little bundle on the sleeping bag—her jeans, Miss Willie's shirtwaist, and, funny, sad, the Braves tie on his scrawny neck. Mr. Renty's eyes were closed and he breathed heavily.

Kate sat down on the ground to catch her breath and put a hand on his forehead. It was burning hot.

"Mr. Renty?" she said. "It's Kate. How do you feel?"

The blue eyes, the merry wise blue eyes, opened glazed and unseeing, and closed once again.

"I'm getting you out of here," Kate said, not knowing how she was going to manage it, but knowing she had to do it.

She looked at the path she had come up. It was crooked and rough but all downhill. She reached to the little man and wrapped the sleeping bag around him.

"Hang on," she said. "I'm gon' pull you down to the river. If I get you that far, I can get help pretty fast. Hang on."

The little man gave no indication of having heard her. Kate gently rolled him into the center of the bag and zipped it around him. She eased the bag to the edge of the slope and knelt on the mossy ground. *I'm not gon' make it*, she thought. And then, *You got to.*

Little by little she eased the big bundle down the slope, supporting the old man's head to keep it from falling backward, until the ground leveled off a bit. Then she stood and grasped one end of the sleeping bag, the end where the little man's head turned restlessly, and lifting it, she tugged. The padded nylon caught on the branches of little bushes and was stopped once by a rock in its downward progress along the path. Kate unsnagged brambles and rolled rocks out of the way. The old man moaned faintly.

"Hang on," Kate urged. "Help's not far now."

The last slope to the riverside was smoother but steep, and Kate was afraid her bundle would start slipping and fall into the river. She leaned over and took it in her arms. Mr. Renty weighed no more than a child and the sleeping bag was light. But her arms and back ached and she stumbled a little before she attained the smooth stretch of sand the children called the beach. She laid the old man down gently and stood a moment, breathing hard. She dared not try to carry him across the river. The rocks were slippery and there were spots where the water ran deep. If she fell with him, it might kill him.

Pneumonia, thought Kate. *I bet he's got pneumonia. I can't dunk him in the river.*

Catching her breath, she took off her shoes again and knelt down to smooth the old man's still fluffy white hair.

"You be sweet and stay right here," she said. "Kate's gon' bring you some blueberries."

Even the mention of his favorite blueberries failed to get a flicker of response from the old man. Kate hoped that meant he would not try to struggle up and get away before she returned with help. She had no idea what she would do when she got across the river, but houses and telephones couldn't be too far away. She would drive to the nearest and call for help.

Kate had backed her car around into a small clearing at the top of the slope. As she climbed up from the river, she saw that the front door on the driver's side was open and a pair of blue-jeaned legs protruded from it. She ran toward the car. There was a man, young, teenage, leaning in under the dash, and there was another inside.

Oh, God, she thought. *Car thieves. Murderers, robbers, rapists!*

"Hi, boys!" she called in a voice that sounded to her unnaturally shrill. "Don't hotwire it! I have the keys."

The knees came out and a tall boy with long greasy black hair and a sharp wolfish face emerged.

"Well, here's the chick," he said, taking a crumpled nubbin of cigarette out of his mouth and handing it to the one who was now scrambling out of the car.

"Thanks," said Kate with a boldness she didn't feel. "I haven't been a chick since 'Hector was a pup.' But I'm glad to see you all. Come on, I need you. There's an old man across the river we've got to get to the hospital."

The second boy, short and blond, stood on the ground. He handed the dirty cigarette back to the tall dark one and hitched up his jeans. Both of them were bare from the waist up.

"Don't just stand there!" commanded Kate crossly. "We've got to hurry. He may die. Come on, I'll show you!"

Surprisingly, they followed her, slow-footed and reluctant at first and then faster, probably impelled by curiosity. She didn't like having them at her back.

At the edge of the river Kate suggested that they take off their shoes.

"Naw," said the older one, grinning wolfishly. "Keep 'em on for running in case I fall into a trap."

"The very idea!" scoffed Kate. But lest he think she was making fun of him and become offended, she added, "Mr. Eli Renty is the old man. You all live around here, so I'm sure you know him."

"I do," said the younger one.

"I'm afraid he's bad sick," Kate said. "We might save his life if we hurry."

They hurried, sliding down the bank and into the water. Kate followed more cautiously. Mr. Renty was where she had left him, breathing loudly.

"Pick him up easy, boys," Kate said. "One of you take his shoulders, one his legs. Support his back. Don't drop him in the water!"

They did as she directed and Kate marveled inwardly.

They were probably young criminals, but they were almost tender in their handling of the old man. She followed them, the rocks cutting and bruising her bare feet. On the bank she went ahead and opened the back door of the car.

"Put him here," she said, and then, daringly, hoping for their continued helpfulness, "I'll sit back here and hold him. One of you drive. Which one is the better driver?"

"He thinks he is," said the blond one, jerking a thumb at the older one.

"Okay," said Kate. "You know the way to the north Fulton hospital?"

"Damn right," said the kid, hitching up his jeans and climbing manfully into the front seat. The blond one followed on the other side.

"By the way," said Kate, taking Mr. Renty's head in her lap, "I'm Kate Mulcay. What are your names?"

"Theron Tippens," mumbled the younger one. "He's Clarence Wiggins."

"Oh, of course!" said Kate. "I bet I know your parents. I'm so glad you came to the rescue!" Inwardly she prayed, *Don't let them dump Mr. Renty and me by the roadside and steal the company car!*

Clarence drove speedily but competently up to the paved road and on to the new community hospital.

At the entrance to the emergency room the boys stood by the car, uneasy spectators, while a hospital crew lifted Mr. Renty onto a rolling stretcher, covered him with a sheet, and wheeled him toward the sliding doors. His Braves tie fell to one side and the boys, seeing it, looked at one another in amusement.

"Goddamn, a Braves fan!" said the older one.

"Pitches for them," said the younger one, grinning.

Kate followed the stretcher to the emergency room and stopped at a desk to give such information as she had. Eli Renty, eighty-odd years old, lives in Cherokee County. She did not know how he was hurt. Found him on a walk in the woods not far from her house. She did not know his Social Security number. Next of kin? She was vague about that, purposely not mentioning Charlene. Who will be responsible for his bill? She was even vaguer. She herself would pay for the immediate emergency room charge, but if he needed prolonged care—at, say, $1,000 a day—she couldn't handle it.

Kate decided he would have to be transferred to Grady Hospital downtown, the old city-county hospital which had always been the refuge of the poor and which Kate loved dearly from having covered it as a reporter.

The starchy young woman behind the desk was not pleased with Kate's answers but, apparently deciding she was hopeless, let her go to the emergency waiting room. The few relatives and friends waiting out some emergency treatment were mostly young and well dressed but as anxious and restless as Kate herself. Unable to settle down and read a magazine, she paced the many-windowed room and occasionally peered out of one to check on the borrowed car and the two boys.

Once she thought the car was missing, and she walked to another window for a better view as a young doctor in surgical green nylon came out of the emergency room and called her name.

Mr. Renty, he said, apparently had serious internal injuries, severe bleeding, and a possible ruptured spleen, possible kidney damage. He would have to be hospitalized for further examination and possible surgery.

Did Kate know how he had been injured?

Kate swallowed hard, aware of her muddy skirt, briar-scratched bare legs, and dirty, sweaty face. She shook her head.

"I think he suffered a severe beating," the young doctor said with sudden decision. "This means I will have to call the police."

Kate knew she should have called the police again in spite of her annoyance with their incompetence. But getting him from under the Big Rock, down the hill, and across the river had consumed her attention as well as her strength. Not to mention having to enlist the help of two probable marijuana-smoking young criminals.

She nodded mutely.

The doctor moved quickly to the admissions desk and picked up a phone. He spoke to a security man somewhere in the hospital and hung up, turning to Kate. "I'm going to have to ask you to wait in here until the police arrive," he said firmly.

Kate should have said she planned to, but instead said humbly, "May I see him?" nodding toward the closed door.

The doctor was reluctant.

"He's not really conscious. We gave him something for pain." But looking at the anxiety on Kate's smudged face, he said, "Okay. For a minute."

The little man lay so quiet and still under the hospital sheet. They had washed his face and hands and there was a tube in his nose and one taped to his wrist. His Braves necktie had been removed along with Kate's jeans and Miss Willie's shirtwaist and was substituted with a hospital gown. Kate held his free hand for a moment and whispered his name. He did not respond.

"Bad?" she whispered to the doctor on the other side of the table.

He nodded. "Are you related?"

"No. Neighbors," said Kate. Tears welled up in her eyes and she turned away. Little bouncy, funny man, as much a part of her life in the country as the red fox she saw in the road at twilight or the guineas that patrolled her yard now and then. She didn't want to lose him.

She started toward the little room the doctor had indicated as a sort of detention cell for people the police needed to see. At that moment two county policemen who had apparently been in the neighborhood walked in.

"Well, Kate, whatcha got for us?" Rufus Burch asked.

She smiled wanly at the pair and indicated the doctor. "My old neighbor, Mr. Renty—you know Mr. Renty?—has been hurt. Dr. . . ." She glanced at his name tag. "Dr. Price here thinks he has been badly beaten."

Surprised that she had taken the matter of talking to the police out of his hands and was apparently already known to them, the young doctor looked abashed. But he rallied.

"Bruises, lacerations, contusions, internal injuries, possible kidney and spleen damage," he said.

"All right, Kate," said Patrolman Burch, taking out his notebook and pen, "who did it?"

Kate glanced at the doctor. "I don't know, but you know who I suspect—his niece Charlene and her boyfriend. Anyhow, I guess she is his next of kin and should be notified."

The two officers wanted to see the victim and Dr.

Price led them to the treatment room. Kate waited while they went in, and studied their faces when they came out—shock and pity.

They said they knew the old Renty place and would ask help from Cherokee County police in finding Charlene, who was still missing. Meanwhile, Mr. Renty was being prepared to be transferred to Grady Hospital.

"Hasn't got a dime," Rufus Burch said. "Steals stuff to eat out of people's gardens."

Kate didn't like the word *steal*, but she admitted to herself that it was applicable. The ambulance crew would not come to get Mr. Renty until his condition had been stabilized, the young doctor said. He was already getting a blood transfusion and would probably need another one. It might be nighttime before the transfer was made.

"Then I'll go home and come back," Kate said.

She had forgotten all about transportation. Where was the staff car?

Reaching the parking lot, Kate noticed the staff car wasn't where they had parked to unload Mr. Renty. She had a sinking spell. The pseudo-Samaritans, almost certainly car thieves, had made off with the company's car. She had even made it easy for them by leaving the key in the ignition. She was on the verge of calling for help from the two policemen who walked along beside her toward their patrol car when she saw it. And leaning into the engine with the hood up were Clarence and Theron.

"Say, fellers," said Officer Burch, "watcha think you're doing there? That's Mrs. Mulcay's car."

"Think so?" said Clarence of the long hair and lupine face, straightening up and grinning at the officers.

Theron, clearly nervous, threw Kate an appealing look. "We know, sir. We just a-lookin'."

"You better come with us," suggested Officer Putnam quietly. "I think we got a record on you two already."

"No, wait!" cried Kate. "These are good boys. They helped me get Mr. Renty across the river and to the hospital. I couldn't have got him here without them. Clarence drove and he must have heard a knock or something in my car."

"Right," said Clarence, grinning. "Your bepteto axmore was missing. I fixed it."

The officers looked perplexed but relieved. "Okay, Kate," Patrolman Burch said. "If you vouch for them."

"Oh, I do!" said Kate. "They're my friends—and good ones."

The policemen went to their car and Kate got in hers. "Come on, boys," she said. "I'll take you home."

"Thanks, chick," said Clarence, climbing into the front seat.

"If you call me 'chick' one more time, I'm gon' bop you one," said Kate irritably. "You call me Miss Kate. I expect I'm as old as your mother. 'Chick's' not respectful."

The lean saytr face was bewildered. *Respect* was obviously not a word in his vocabulary.

"Yes'm," he said meekly. And then as an afterthought, "How's the old man?"

"Pretty bad," Kate said.

"I reckon he's gon' die," remarked Theron from the backseat. "Mommer's gon' hate it. They're kin."

Kin? She was surprised to hear that Mr. Renty had any kin outside of Charlene.

"Well, you all brought him where he can be helped,"

Kate said. "If he lives, it'll be because you all did that."

Kate let them out at a tarpaper-covered shack she had not noticed before, tucked under the approach to the bridge—an old fishing camp, she thought. They probably hung out there by themselves, but she saw a tendril of smoke drifting up as blue as morning glories from a brick flue and smelled fish frying.

"Mommer's home, musta caught supper," remarked Theron. "Fishes all the time and don't ketch much. Today musta been different."

Kate smiled at his pride and backed around to get back on the paved road. The frying fish did smell good. She remembered she had not eaten all day.

It might have been useful leaving her car with Edge and Bambi. At least they would have something to cook in the house, if they had not already cooked it.

When she turned into her own driveway, she saw smoke billowing up from the backyard. She parked hastily and hurried toward the house, slowing down when she saw it was her outdoor cooker. They had been barbecuing. The Greens and the across-the-road neighbors were seated at the picnic table with paper plates before them.

"Hi, Cuz!" called Edge, getting up to meet her. "Hope you've eaten. You're late for the ribs. But let me get you a drink. Bets and Bob are here," he added unnecessarily.

Kate smiled and waved at them and put an arm around Shawn's shoulders, glad to notice that he did not draw away this time, but looked up from his seat at the picnic table and smiled shyly.

"You didn't call us to meet your bus," Bambi began accusingly, and stopped.

"I had a job up this way and got a company car," Kate said. "I should have called anyhow. I'm sorry."

"Well, it's your loss," mumbled Bambi. "We ate your supper."

"Did we?" asked Bets anxiously. "I thought I might have eaten your share. But Edge said there were plenty of ribs."

Edge came out of the kitchen bearing a glass half full of an amber liquor. "Scotch," he said. "Water okay? We're out of soda."

"Water's fine," Kate said, "but keep it for me until I can change my clothes. I've been out in the woods and I'm a mess."

"Sure," said Edge. "I'll guard it from Bambi and Bob till you get back." He laughed expansively at his own joke.

Scotch, Kate mused as she ran upstairs. *I didn't have any Scotch. Can't afford it. They used the grocery money. They'll have to have even more money tomorrow.*

Kate wanted a leisurely soak in the tub, but she took a quick shower instead and pulled on some jeans and a T-shirt and, carrying her sneakers in her hands, went back to the yard.

She took a seat by Shawn and accepted the drink Edge pushed toward her without interrupting a story he was telling. She was hungry and she hated scotch, but in deference to the guests she would drink it and get a peanut butter sandwich later.

Looking at the Dunns now, she thought they were an oddly disparate couple. Bob was extremely handsome, tall and lean with a shock of dark hair laced with silver, and black eyebrows. He had very white teeth in a suntanned face. He had mentioned that he played tennis at the subdivision's clubhouse. Bets was thin—on the wiry side rather than slender—and she had a gamine haircut that was unbecoming, back and sides shingled to a topknot of brown hair, which lay limp and dispirited close to her skull. Her ears were big and stuck out prominently like the ears on a pitcher. Her face, wrinkled by age or too much sun, tried to rally with a too-bright slash of lipstick. Her eyes, back behind harlequin glasses, rested anxiously on the decimated rib platter.

Kate smiled at the plain woman. No beauty herself, she felt a sense of kinship with Bets, though she wondered sometimes how they had got together—the handsome man who was laughing at some remark from Edge, and Bets who was nice but not much to look at. Kate had come to value Bets—in spite of her wariness about subdivision people—because of her interest in country history and her pleasure in the country. Bets had become friends with Miss Willie and she borrowed wildflower books from Kate, dropping by occasionally with a sprig or a few leaves to ask help in identifying an interesting plant.

Besides, Kate told herself with a little inward sigh, all the clichés about beauty did seem to apply—pretty is as pretty does, beauty is in the eye of the beholder, and perhaps the most discouraging of all, a saying from Miss Willie: Pretty ugly and pretty apt to stay that way. As for herself, she had been comforted by a line by Elinor Wylie when she had a husband who was better looking than she was: "Say not of beauty she is good/ Or aught but beautiful."

Benjy, fortunately, seemed unaware that he was macho handsome while Kate, with her skinny young body, carroty hair, and freckles, looked, as a loathsome boy in high school once told her, like a "pale glass of lemonade."

Maybe it was the same with Bob, she thought doubtfully, looking at him as he moved from the picnic bench to a chair by the hammock.

Bets saw him move and said softly to Kate, "I've been wanting to talk to you."

"How about now?" said Kate with a quick glance at Bob, who seemed to shift focus from some prattle of Bambi's to a sudden interest in Bets and Kate.

"I'm embarrassed to ask you," Bets said. "But I don't know the difference between *crenate* and *dentate.*"

"You're not so stupid you can't look that up in the dictionary," Bob said brusquely.

"Ah, but Bets is coming to the old wildflower master!" Kate said brightly. "Now, crenate leaves are scalloped, sort of. And dentate leaves, as the word suggests, are sort of toothy—pointed, really. You're not into foamflowers, are you?"

"Sure," said Bets. "Lots of them from Miss Willie's creek bank. But I call them," she said smugly, "false miterwort. It's the saxifrage your book says is blooming now that I can't find."

Bob's attention wandered back to Bambi, and Kate promised to take a walk in the woods with Bets on her next day off. She had a feeling they had averted something unpleasant and was anxious to know what Bets really had to say.

She had not told anybody except Miss Willie about Mr. Renty for fear that Charlene and her boyfriend would come asking for him and they would disclose his whereabouts. She considered telling them now, but then the Gandy sisters came racing into the yard.

It was the way they often traveled, racing one another from house to house, and the marvel was that the older and slightly bigger one, Sheena, did not always win.

Now they puffed up to the picnic table, their young eyes checking both it and the boy Shawn who sat there.

"Miss Kate, did he die? Mommer said," demanded Sheena peremptorily, unconcerned that she might be interrupting adult conversation.

Kate reached out an arm and pulled the girl close. The feeling in the country had once been that people only went to a hospital to die. The Gandys should have known better, since their father, prone to drink and wrecking cars, spent considerable time in a hospital.

"Did he, did he die?" put in Kim Sue.

Kate shook her head. "No, honey, he's gon' be better, I hope. How did you all know he was in the hospital?"

"Our aint, mommer's sister, she was there with her least young'un and she seen him."

"Saw him," Kate corrected automatically.

"Who are they talking about?" Bets asked. "Anybody we know?"

"I don't know if you know old Mr. Renty," Kate said. "He's a funny little man who roams the countryside. He was hurt somehow and couldn't go home. We took him to the hospital."

Bets said with undue firmness, "No, we don't know him." Kate may have imagined it, but she thought she saw Bets and Bob exchange glances.

"Aw, somebody beat him up," Sheena said darkly,

reaching for a potato chip. "Me and Miss Kate knows that, don't we, Miss Kate?"

"Probably deserved it," mumbled Bambi drowsily.

Kate looked at her. She was slumped down in the yard chair, obviously drunk.

"Peeping Tom, I bet," Bambi added to herself.

Maybe it was weariness or hunger or worry over Mr. Renty, but Kate felt a sudden surge of anger.

"If I find out who beat him, I'll kill them!" she said furiously.

The Gandy sisters looked delighted, but the grown-ups began to stir uneasily, stacking paper plates and finishing their drinks. The party seemed to be over. The Dunns thanked Edge and Bambi and headed back across the road. Edge grasped Bambi's hands and pulled her to her feet. "Beddy, beddy," he murmured.

Kate sat on, sipping the horrid scotch and watching the Gandys wolf down the leftover potato chips and pickles. Shawn, followed by Pepper, wandered off to watch the guineas, which were flapping into the big pear tree one at a time, early to roost. The Gandys went to join him.

After a time, Edge came out of the house and sat on the corner of the picnic table nearest Kate.

"I hope you don't mind we had that little party," he said. "Them people across the road was nice to us and they told Bambi you are too busy to swap invitations. She thought it would be okay with you if we had a little cookout. Ribs is cheap right now and I flatter myself I know how to barbecue them just right."

"I'm sure they were good," Kate said. "And the scotch," she added venomously, knowing it was not kind to ask for an accounting.

Edge's attention wandered to the guineas.

"Beer woulda suited you and me," he said. "But Bambi said the Dunns had scotch and she thought we ought to."

Besides, she gets drunk faster on scotch than on beer, Kate said to herself.

"You had money enough?" she asked, figuring how far you could go with $30.

"Just did," said Edge. "We kinda out of groceries right now."

Kate sighed. "I'll get a check cashed tomorrow."

She stood up. "Now I'd better call the office and the hospital."

When Kate called the office, Shell had gone for the day and the night city editor hadn't even known that Kate had a staff car, so he said, "Keep it. Bring it back tomorrow." Somebody in the emergency room at the hospital said Mr. Renty's condition was "stable" and that he had been transferred to Grady. The county police said they had not found anybody at the old Renty place, so there still hadn't been any notification of kinfolks.

Kate longed for bed, although the setting sun still streaked the western horizon with bands of rose and gold, and a pearly light lingered over the yard. The Gandy sisters and Shawn galloped over the grass in pursuit of lightning bugs.

The blue hour, Kate said to herself. *Savor it instead of giving way to self-pity and the wrongnesses.* On impulse she pulled a disc out of the stack on the old pie safe, which housed her tapes and CD player. (She refused to call it an "entertainment center.") It was a Mozart requiem but one that comforted and seemed to celebrate life. She turned it on softly and stretched out on the sofa.

* * *

When Kate awakened, Shawn was asleep on the roll-away bed, the cat Sugar slept on Kate's feet, and she was still in her jeans and sneakers. Another day had dawned.

Before she left for work, Kate checked the cupboards for supplies. The peanut butter jar was empty. Bacon and eggs nonexistent. A shriveled carrot and two potatoes constituted the vegetable stock. Even the new scotch bottle was in the recycle bin—empty. Poor things, she thought, no food. She wrote a check for $100 and put it under a glass on the kitchen table. As an afterthought she made a list to go along with the check—a pot roast, vegetables, milk, bread, butter, eggs, pet food for Pepper and Sugar, cookies for Shawn, and peanut butter, her personal standby when all else failed. If she were doing the shopping herself, she would also get Cokes and possibly a six-pack of beer, but she did not want to encourage Bambi's drinking, which she now knew was serious.

The morning paper was on the front steps, and after a cursory glance at the front page she opened it to the want ads and put it on the kitchen table beside the check and the grocery list. The Greens still slept.

Before she returned the staff car, Kate thought she had better stop by Grady Hospital and check on Mr. Renty. The little man was asleep, looking more childish than ever in his blue hospital gown. A young intern told her he had had a restless night and was in a lot of pain. They had raised the sides of his bed to keep him from falling out, of course, but Kate regarded the shiny bars sadly. They symbolized imprisonment for the freest person she knew.

She was glad, however, to have her friend in the arms of old Grady Hospital. But to have him needing to be there was distressing. He should be roaming the woods, wading creeks, raiding orchards.

"What did you find in the way of internal injuries?" she asked the young doctor. He looked at the chart in his hand and said briefly, "Ruptured spleen. He will need surgery. Do you know how to reach family members?"

Kate shook her head. "There's only a niece—and I don't know where she is." *And if I did know,* she thought, *I wouldn't tell her.* "Can't you go on with the operation?"

"I'm afraid not. We have to have authorization. If you can find next of kin, will you let us know? Better still, ask them to come in to the hospital."

And bring a battling stick and finish the job, Kate thought bitterly.

She asked if there was anything else she could do, if Mr. Renty needed toilet articles or pajamas, which he clearly did not. Still, Kate wanted to feel useful. She left her name and her telephone numbers, patted the little hand, which was immobilized with an IV, and left.

Kate sipped coffee from a Styrofoam cup and read her mail, neglected because of matters at home and worries over Mr. Renty. A prisoner, wrongly accused of breaking and entering, wrote from a public works camp, where he was getting blisters on his hands from working on the roads. He was a violinist, he said, and would never play again when the state of Georgia got through with him. Kate put in a call to the Department of Corrections to get his history.

An elderly woman whose Social Security check was days late wanted somebody to speak to the government on her behalf. The woman suspected her mailman of thievery. A garden club wanted Kate to speak. A home for AIDS patients wanted her to join a fund-raising campaign.

The checkout girl at a supermarket had been rude to a customer, who was, she said, fighting mad—and did Kate blame her? A man who did spectacular wood carvings wanted an appointment to bring them in and show them to Kate. Object: Publicity.

And so it went. By noon Kate was half asleep from the problems of other people and had not had time to write a column or tackle the problems that beset her. How could she move Edge and Bambi out of her house? How could she find Charlene and get the operation Mr. Renty needed?

Somehow she got a column written and by four o'clock was ready to call Edge and ask him to meet her at the MARTA stop in Alpharetta. Shell took her word for it that there wasn't much of a story in Mr. Renty's beating.

"Wait till it turns into a murder, Kate," he said lightly. "That's when you can spin into action."

Kate couldn't think beyond Mr. Renty's injuries. If he died, she thought, it would be murder. And by whom? She suspected Charlene, but she had no evidence and the old man would not name names.

She called the hospital before she left for the MARTA train, and the cliché about Mr. Renty's condition being "fair" didn't hearten her at all. Better she should get home, get her car, and head for the old Renty house across the river.

Edge and Shawn met her at the park-ride lot when she got off the MARTA bus. Edge was quieter than usual and appeared dejected. Shawn, on the other hand, was livelier than usual.

"Look what I got, Cuz'n Kate!" he said. "Seeds! I'm gon' plant a garden. Miss Willie gave them to me. She says it's just about time to plant turnips and collards and she said one time she had good luck planting beans this late. You like beans, Cuz'n Kate?"

"Love 'em," said Kate. "Did Miss Willie tell you where to plant them and how?"

"Sure did!" said Shawn. "That time she had good luck she said she had bean seeds left over and she just scattered them in the shade at the edge of her garden. And boy, they come up and made bushels of beans!"

"Wonderful," said Kate. "Miss Willie knows about things like that. Do you like beans?"

The little boy looked guilty. "No, ma'am," he said.

Kate and Edge laughed. "That's all right," Kate said. "The rest of us will eat them."

When they got home, there appeared to be trouble in the house. Bambi was in bed. She had a hangover, Edge confided, "and none of the hair of the dog that bit her."

"Oh, my," said Kate, "and I don't suppose you had enough money left over for even medicinal whiskey?"

"Nope," said Edge. "It was a big list."

Kate was about to apologize, although she didn't feel apologetic, when Bambi called for Edge. He hurried up the stairs and came back in a moment looking purposeful. "I'm going to run over to the Dunns'," he said. "Bambi pointed out that we didn't have any garlic for the roast. I'll borrow some."

Kate nodded. He was out of the yard and across the road when she thought to look at the little wire basket hanging over the sink where she kept garlic. It had two fine fat bulbs in it. She wouldn't embarrass Edge by calling him back when she was certain he was going to borrow at least a cup of scotch. *Poor things,* she thought once more. *It must be hell to be so dependent.*

The roast smelled good and she lifted a pot lid and saw that the beans and potatoes were done. Somebody in the Green family was apparently a competent cook.

Shawn sat on the back steps sifting some tiny black seeds through his fingers, looking dreamily absorbed. In a little while the Gandy sisters arrived barefoot and wearing their most disreputable cut-off, bleach-spotted jeans.

"Come on, Shawn," Sheena commanded. "You want to build a dam we got to hurry before it gits dark."

They trotted off toward Miss Willie's creek with Pepper following.

Kate decided she better hurry to have time for a run over to the old Renty house and get back before supper. Charlene might be there—or somebody who would qualify to give permission for the spleen operation on Mr. Renty.

Kate parked on the shoulder of the road in front of the snaggletoothed picket fence. There were no stuffed animals arranged in front of it today, but she noticed as she walked up to the front porch that the man-sized bear with the violin was still there, leering at her. The house and yard were silent. The front door appeared to be locked. Kate walked around to the side of the house looking for a car, but there was none there. She stood a moment in the tall grass listening to the silence. It wasn't really eerie, but when a whippoorwill sounded back in the woods, she shivered involuntarily.

The old house had a long-gone air about it. Charlene and her boyfriend might be hundreds of miles away.

She was glad that her car started promptly and she lurched down the rutted road, relieved to be going home, even if it no longer seemed to be her home.

Edge had apparently forgotten the garlic and in truth brought a medicinal shot of whiskey for Bambi. She sat on a chair in the yard in the shade of the maple tree and drank it in a grateful gulp. With an expression of distaste on her plump face, which appeared naked without its customary coat of makeup, Bambi watched Kate cross the yard.

I don't think she likes me, Kate said to herself, amused. As a matter of fact, even Edge seemed uncomfortable with her. Only Shawn, patient, brooding, had relaxed a bit and settled contentedly into the little cabin and its surroundings. Miss Willie and the Gandy sisters were responsible. They had so many projects to interest a boy, planting a garden, building a dam.

Bambi was plainly bored and poor Edge, striving mightily to earn his keep, kept doing all the wrong things, Kate thought, her eyes falling on the decimated thicket she had loved and nurtured for so many years. She would try to be nicer. She herself had been self-supporting for so many years that she could not imagine what it would be like to show up jobless and accept some stranger's charity. A stranger, she thought wryly, who didn't even keep scotch in the house.

The next day, counting it an emergency, Grady doctors removed Mr. Renty's spleen. Kate sat out the operation in the family waiting room. It seemed unbearably sad to her that he had no real family to care whether he lived or died. She was probably his favorite stranger, but a stranger nonetheless. When the operation was over and the little man was in the recovery room, Kate returned to work. At the end of the day, before she caught the MARTA train for home, she walked back to the hospital along Decatur Street, stopping at one of the little sidewalk stands that had sprung up downtown, to get Mr. Renty a basket of fruit. He probably couldn't eat it anyhow, so it was all right that there were no blueberries in it. It would cheer him to see it, she hoped. Decatur Street had been her favorite downtown street before it was slum-cleared to make way for Georgia State University's pristine white blocky buildings and interspersed with parking garages.

In her early days as a reporter for the *Atlanta Searchlight*, Kate had walked down that street every day to the police station press room and to Grady Hospital. It had been a shabby old street of pawnshops, secondhand furniture stores, and catfish and pork chop restaurants. Used dresses and suits on hangers, hanging from doorways, flapped and turned in incongruous dances. A peanut roaster whistled in front of a hardware store. There was a shop where you could buy High John the Conqueror roots, genseng, and love and luck potions. It always amused Kate that some federal agency had required the vendors to put labels on packages specifying that these were "alleged" love and luck potions.

She loved Decatur Street and made friends with more than one merchant. Mr. Walter Bailey was a gentle man whose family had run their hardware store since the early days when wagon trains came down from the mountains to sell hogs and turkeys. She bought wooden butter molds from him and a cedar water bucket. There was a quiet scholarly man who lived upstairs in one of the rooms over a Decatur Street store and grew grapes in the hard-packed backyard. He brought Kate a basket of sweet purple Concords at one summer's ending. The old theater where Bessie Smith had sung the blues was still there and in the middle of the street where Central Avenue intersected Decatur, there was a traffic island populated every morning by half a dozen or more men, both black and white. It was called Hungry Corner and it was where unemployed men went and waited for some Atlantan needing a worker to come by and hire them. By afternoon the island was vacant. The men had either gotten jobs or gone home.

Kate could barely forgive the city for changing Decatur Street. But then she considered what Georgia State University meant to the great middle class of working youngsters who could not afford to go away to school. They filled the MARTA trains and buses every day with their backpacks of books and, oblivious to their surroundings, bent their fresh young faces over notebooks of unfinished outlines or reports. Ponytailed and sometimes bearded boys and young girls with frizzy hair and clunking running shoes poured into trains and buses and marched from Five Points station, a hopeful young army, to the white citadel of learning on Decatur Street. Only a mossbacked diehard would rather have the old Decatur Street than the new one with its library and science building and its beautifully landscaped entranceways. But it just wasn't *interesting,* Kate reflected as she walked toward the hospital. It did not have—she gave herself a for-instance—the fragrance of roasting coffee that used to pour out of a wholesale grocer's. Now the street was splendidly austere, with no suggestion of the shabby, colorful human beings who once populated it.

Mr. Renty was awake when Kate arrived at the hospital. They had moved him to a room and he was perched on the bed like an unfeathered sparrow.

"Do they allow you to sit up like that?" Kate asked, surprised.

"Ain't no allow to it," Mr. Renty answered with spirit. "If you'll hand me my britches, I'm a-going away from here."

"Oh, good!" Kate laughed. "I'm glad you're feeling that pert. But you gon' have to wait a spell. When they tell you to go, I'll bring the car and take you home."

"I can walk," said the old man stubbornly.

"Ha!" said Kate. "You're pretty feisty, all right, but I'd hate to see you hobbling through downtown traffic."

"Where's my necktie?" the old man demanded suddenly, as if it were a talisman that would give him strength.

"I'll ask them to bring it to you, but I doubt if it's hospital-clean. You may have to wait to wear it. Meanwhile, can I peel one of these oranges for you?"

Mr. Renty had not noticed the basket of fruit and his blue eyes became incandescent. His old hands reached out and lovingly smoothed the skins of the apples and caressed the golden shape of the bananas. Kate went outside to the nurses' station to see if he was allowed to eat the fruit and came back to find him diligently peeling and dividing orange segments.

She laughed and felt more cheerful than she had in days. The cuts and bruises on his face were healing and he *seemed* well.

After finishing his orange, Mr. Renty lay back against a

pillow and crushed and inhaled the fragrance of the orange peels. Kate asked conversationally, "Mr. Renty, who beat you up so bad?"

"Ask me no questions and I'll tell you no lies!" he said impudently.

"Now, Mr. Renty, sir," Kate said reprovingly, "that's sassy of you. I just want to be sure that when you go home you'll go to a safe place where nobody will hurt you. There's no call for you to be rude to me."

His old face clouded over like a scolded child's. "I don't mean you no disrespect," he said. "I cain't . . . I cain't . . ." He stopped and tucked his chin into the hospital gown and closed his eyes.

He's scared, Kate thought. *He's scared to death.* She felt ashamed of herself.

"It's okay, Mr. Renty," she said, reaching for his hand. "Anybody hurt you again, I'll kill 'em dead."

All the Greens—Edge, Bambi, and Shawn—met Kate at the MARTA park-ride lot. Shawn was interested in the big buses and Edge had walked around with him to look at the ones that had ten- or fifteen-minute waits. The drivers were obliging about letting passengers who debarked there in the wintertime wait inside the warm bus if their rides were slow to pick them up. The same in the summertime, when the sun beat on the asphalt of the parking lot and the bus was the only air-conditioned thing in sight. Today they were pleased that Edge and his son wanted to inspect the buses. The drivers showed off their slick vinyl interiors with pride.

Bambi obviously had a different thing on her mind. She was almost sober and very cordial to Kate, asking her what kind of day she had had and if she was tired, matters that had not interested her before.

When Edge and Shawn returned to the car, Kate was a little surprised that Edge opened the back door for her and Shawn and took the driver's seat for himself next to Bambi. It wasn't that she minded not driving, she thought, but it seemed like yet another blatant example of their takeover.

Bambi half turned from the front seat and said meltingly, "The Dunns invited us to a dinner party!"

"You, too," said Edge. "They want you, too. It's Saturday night."

Dear Lord, what next? Kate said to herself. There's no limit to things to be done. The Dunns were fine. She liked them all right. But did she have to break bread with them every night of the week?

Bambi seemed chagrined that Kate hadn't answered right away and rested her chin on the back of her seat and pouted.

"You don't want to go," she said accusingly. "All the subdivision people are going to be there and they wanted you especially."

I wonder why, Kate mused. *We have a live-and-let-live policy, don't we? Why this sudden urge to meet and eat?*

Edge answered the unspoken question.

"I think they like Bambi. They wanted her especially and just asked us to go along. Shawn is invited, too. They have a swimming pool, you know, and we're supposed to bring our suits."

Oh, Lordy. Kate sighed.

"I think it's lovely," she said at last. "Of course you all must go. I'm not sure I can. I have an assignment."

"The other thing," said Bambi, ignoring the fact that Kate was trying to make her regrets, "is that it's going to be dressy. I didn't bring anything like that to wear. I noticed in your closet that you have several dressy dresses—dinner dresses and an evening dress and such. Of course, I can't wear your things, but . . ."

"What she wants to say, Cuz'n," put in Edge, "is will you stake her a few dollars for a dress? We'll pay you back, of course."

Kate took a deep breath and let it out slowly. She wanted to say, *What do you mean probing around in my closet?*, but she looked at Shawn's worried young face and said instead, "I'll be glad to let you use my credit card, Bambi, but I really doubt that you have to dress up for a neighborhood party. People out here are pretty casual."

"How do you know?" Bambi asked petulantly. "Bets said you never go to parties."

Kate sighed. They were right to charge her with unsociability. She went to work. She came home. She read or wrote or worked in her yard. She occasionally went to the symphony or to something at the historical society. She went to church and, if pushed, would go with a friend to a movie. But she didn't go to parties.

I'm drawing in, instead of reaching out, she admitted. *I may be like Charlene said, drying up. I may be like that old-guard Atlantan who said, "We HAVE our friends."*

"Okay," she capitulated. "I'll try to make this one." She fumbled in her bag and handed Bambi her credit card.

Edge and Bambi looked at one another happily. "If it's okay with you," Edge said, "we'll drop you off and come back to the mall. Or do you want to go with us up to North Point?"

Kate shook her head. "No, thank you. I'm a little tired. I think I'll go on home."

That's one more thing, she thought. She hated shopping. There was this glorious new mall over by the old public works camp and she had been in it for half an hour one day shortly after it opened. It was beautiful and offered treasures from all over the world. It had a glass elevator she hoped one day to get Miss Willie in for the fun of seeing the old lady's reaction. But no, she didn't want to go shopping.

Shawn got out, too, when they reached the cabin. "Don't you want to go shopping with them?" Kate asked.

He wrinkled his nose, which was sunburned and peeling a little. "No, ma'am!" he said emphatically. "I promised Miss Willie I'd help her clean out her chicken house."

Kate grinned. It was a recurring chore for the old woman. She wanted the dirt floor under the chicken roost raked and smoothed, but more than that, she wanted the chicken droppings for her garden. This was the season when she began to build up her compost pile.

"I'll go with you," Kate said. "Let me change my clothes."

Half an hour later she sat on Miss Willie's front porch in shorts and sneakers and listened to the creek in the front yard and Shawn's inexpert wielding of shovel and rake in the backyard.

Miss Willie had field peas and okra simmering on the stove and a cake of crackling bread in the oven, and she counted on Kate and Shawn staying for supper.

The peace of the old house and the earth around it entered Kate's bones. She moved the old cowhide-bottomed rocker slowly to and fro with a kind of end-of-the-day, sunset-hour rhythm.

Miss Willie handed her a big jelly glass full of iced tea and took a chair beside her.

"Miss Willie," Kate said after a long, tranquil silence, "what are we going to do with Mr. Renty when the hospital releases him?"

The old woman rocked slowly and was quiet, considering.

"Bring him here," Miss Willie said finally. "I'll see after him."

Kate was delighted. "Would you, Miss Willie? Would you do that? You know I can't. My house is full."

The old lady nodded serenely. "What are neighbors for?" she asked. Kate thought of an answer having to do with other neighbors: Saturday night parties you have to buy fancy dresses for. But she said nothing and reached out for one of Miss Willie's wrinkled, work-roughened old hands and squeezed it.

The peas and okra and the cornbread well flavored with bits of lean pork from Miss Willie's last hog-killing tasted wonderful. Shawn ate two plates full and stretched out on the porch, his hands clasped behind his head.

Kate carried the dishes to the kitchen and plunged them into a dishpan full of hot soapy water, Miss Willie's answer to the automatic dishwasher.

"I don't know when they'll let him go," Kate said. "But I'll give you warning before I bring him over."

"No need to," said Miss Willie. "The spare room is scoured, sheets are clean. I got vittles a-plenty. Bring him on when you ready to."

Kate hugged her and prepared to leave. She thought of

making a joke about Miss Willie's reputation—single woman harboring a single man. But she knew it might embarrass her friend. In her own way, Miss Willie was virginal, an eighty-five-year-old innocent.

Two days later, Kate awakened to realize it was Saturday—the day Mr. Renty could be released from the hospital and the day of the Dunns' dinner party. The sky was gray, threatening rain, the air hot and humid. Kate tiptoed to the bathroom and dressed quietly while the Greens slept. Feeling strangely guilty, she took her car. She had left it with the Greens so often they were beginning to have a distinctly proprietary interest in it. She wouldn't have minded if she had thought Edge was job-hunting, but from the packages she saw on her bed when she eased by to the bathroom, she was certain it was being used for shopping trips. When Kate had asked for her credit card back, Bambi, in a fever of confusion, said she had mislaid it, but Kate was certain Bambi could find it if she wanted to.

Traffic on the expressway was unusually heavy for a Saturday morning, but Kate was glad to take her time anyway. Mr. Renty looked pale getting into her car and she was afraid of shaking him up. She had given him a pillow and a light cover and he had stretched out on the backseat and closed his eyes.

"How would you like a Big Mac for lunch?" Kate asked him.

The old man straightened up and smiled. Kate had bought him blue jeans and a shirt to take the place of his borrowed clothes and she noticed for the first time that he was wearing his necktie. A little dirty, a little crumpled, but smartly tied in a four-in-hand. He mopped at it carefully as he ate his hamburger.

Surprisingly, the old man did not seem to warm up to Miss Willie's hospitality. He entered her old house slowly, almost fearfully, looking around him in wide-eyed discomfort. They decided to take a seat on the porch instead.

"Take a cheer," Miss Willie directed. "I'll fetch you all some tea." Mr. Renty perched on the edge of one of the old porch rockers and looked at Kate anxiously, like a small trapped animal.

Kate and Miss Willie tried to ignore him, drinking their tea and talking of the weather and planting time for such fall crops as turnips and collard greens.

"If you go by Chadwick's," Miss Willie said to Kate, "git me a scattering of radish seed. Mites is bad this year and radishes is good protection for greens."

Kate agreed and asked about Shawn's planting.

"He's got him a garden next to mine," Miss Willie said. "He's a good young'un. He totes water from the well every day to water them rows. I told him when the weather cools off we'll plant some lettuce."

Kate stood by Mr. Renty's chair a moment before leaving. "Don't you think you ought to lie down awhile now? Miss Willie's got you a nice bed in there. A nap might strengthen you."

The old man looked over his shoulder at the door into the front room but said nothing. Kate waited a minute for his answer and looked at Miss Willie.

"You go along," Miss Willie said sturdily. "Me and Mr. Renty will 'bide."

I hope he will abide, Kate thought, walking toward her car. There was simply no other place for him.

* * *

Kate had not given any thought to dressing for the Dunns' party. Her white duck trousers were clean and she had washed her newest sneakers. She had a striped jersey she had never worn and it seemed party-festive, she thought without enthusiasm.

Bambi and Edge were dressed and waiting for her when she emerged from the bathroom. Edge was wearing a dark blue suit, a white shirt, and a tie. Bambi was astonishing in a short bright yellow silk dress and high-heeled slippers to match. She had done something to her hair. It almost matched the dress in color and was a mass of curls.

"My goodness," murmured Kate, inspecting them. "You are dressy."

Edge put an arm around Bambi. "My girl knows how to get herself together for a party," he said proudly. "You gon' get dressed now?"

"I *am* dressed," said Kate, grinning. "This is about as far as I go—unless the Metropolitan Opera is in town."

Bambi turned away in disgust and Kate saw that a major addition to her costume was a foot-wide yellow bow on her fanny. *Lordy, lordy,* Kate said to herself, *Shining Waters Subdivision is gon' be overwhelmed.*

"Where's Shawn?" she asked. "Isn't he going?"

"Aw, he's off playing with them Gandy girls," Edge explained. "He didn't want to go no way."

"Didn't have his good clothes," Bambi put in fretfully, and Kate wondered for the tenth time how much damage Bambi had done to her credit card.

Kate intended to walk to the party. The distance was small, but the little path was steep and rough with loose rocks and briars encroaching along the edge. The Greens were concerned about Bambi's shoes and took the car on the roundabout road leading into the subdivision from the highway. Kate's car was the only one beside the Dunns' in their parking lot, she noticed as she scrambled up the bank from the dirt road. All the other guests seemed to be strolling in from their homes along the subdivision's broad paved and planted walks. They wore shorts and slacks and a couple of guests had terry cloth robes on over their bathing suits.

Kate looked at Bambi and Edge in sympathy.

From a long-ago movie version of Sinclair Lewis's *Dodsworth* she remembered how Ruth Chatterton had insisted on putting on an evening dress for dinner the first night out on shipboard for an Atlantic crossing. Her husband, played by Walter Huston, protested that it was not the custom to dress for dinner on the first night out, but the heroine had said, "I'm sure it's always correct to dress for dinner." She had been alone in her finery and Kate had never forgotten the poor woman's pain.

Now poor little Bambi was the one in pain. She tried to carry it off and Bets Dunn tried to help by admiring her dress extravagantly and calling on the other women who gathered in the kitchen for compliments, but Kate saw Bambi disappear into a bedroom, and when she emerged her face was red from crying.

Eight or ten subdivision residents had assembled and Kate was pleased to see that she knew most of them—a police court judge, an older, silver-haired lawyer, a young doctor, the cute girl who walked a Doberman nearly her size down Kate's road every morning, a man who owned several gas–fast-food stops up near the expressway.

The Dunns had set up a bar on the screened porch

overlooking the swimming pool, where three or four children and a couple of adults splashed about. The dining room that ran the length of the house was such a beautiful room, Kate reflected, looking at the long, many-paned windows, that she caught herself doing what she never expected to do: envying a subdivision dweller. In her cabin she set a table with pottery in the living room or kitchen or, in summer, on the back porch, but it was not a long, shining mahoghany board lit by a crystal chandelier and set with Waterford and Wedgwood like this.

Bob's clocks filled the house—in the dining room, living room, kitchen, basement family room, and on the stair landing. They struck the hour almost but not quite simultaneously.

As she stood admiring a walnut and brass Seth Thomas on a shelf in the breakfast room, Bob came and stood beside her.

"You like clocks, too?" he asked.

"I do," said Kate, "but obviously not with the scope of your affection for them. How many do you have?"

"I have lost count," he said, laughing. "I bought my first one in France right after World War II and I've been picking them up wherever I could find them."

Bets's food was spectacular, Kate decided, chilled avocado soup, followed by some chicken dish that involved Boursin cheese, and platters of fresh vegetables almost too beautiful to eat. She was settling down to enjoy the food when she noticed Bambi's bright head was bobbing toward her plate. Bambi had spent the predinner hour close to the bar on the porch, where Kate thought she was paying more attention to the men than to the drinks. She must have been wrong.

Edge, sitting opposite his wife, had his eyes on her and was clearly concerned.

By the time the strawberry pie was served, Bambi was slumped so far down in her chair, her face was even with the whipped cream. Edge got up on the pretext of helping the hostess and went to his wife's side, whispered something in her ear, and helped her to get up.

They went toward the porch and Kate did not want to call attention to them by following or even appearing to notice. She sipped her wine and kept her attention on the man to her right, who was talking about some public hearing she had missed.

"You are with us, I know," he said to Kate.

Kate thought she should find out where they were, but the man on her left was explaining that the next meeting would be in the high school auditorium and as the oldest—from standpoint of residence, he added charmingly—property owner on the road Kate's appearance would be important.

Kate looked up and everybody at the table seemed to be listening and waiting for her answer. She took another sip of wine and decided to wait them out.

Edge appeared at the door. He had apparently stowed Bambi away on the porch. He was smiling at Kate.

"I think you can count on my cuz'n," he said. "She's for progress." *I am not*, Kate thought stubbornly. *Progress is one of those Mother Hubbard words, covering everything and touching nothing. Progress is the most abused word in the English language. A word used by people who want to destroy.*

"They will, of course, build a new bridge," said Homer Lawton, the police court judge.

"I don't think they'll take more than ten feet off your property, Kate," Bob assured her.

"And think how lovely it will be not to have that dust," said Lucy Aldredge, whose English Tudor mansion backed up to the road directly opposite Kate's house.

Belatedly Kate recognized an old theme. They were talking about the issue she had fought against for twenty years. It had raised its head again! They wanted to pave Loblolly Road. And widen it, and replace the little wooden bridge down across the creek—which rattled companionably when anybody crossed it—with a cold, silent, ugly concrete structure.

Kate stood up and smiled at Bets. "It was a wonderful dinner," she said. "Let me help you clear away."

"Ah, no," said Bets, "Mrs. Gandy's sister is going to come over and clean up for me. But Kate, you haven't answered about the road."

Kate smiled whimsically. "I've been answering that road question for twenty years. I'm opposed to paving Loblolly. I always have been. It may be the last old wagon road left in north Fulton County and I love it as it is. You all have your nice paved streets. You can come in by a paved road. I want to be neighborly, but we need some country left."

Kate took a deep breath. "Your children play on Loblolly Road. Some of you walk your dogs on it. I've seen some of you jogging and biking on it. Why destroy it?"

Down at the end of the table, Cy Hill, the doctor, yawned prodigiously. "Now we're going to get to the possums and the wildflowers," he said.

He was harking back to a movement ten or twelve years ago when Atlanta wanted to build a second airport in north Fulton County. There had been petitions and protest meetings and Kate, to her embarrassment, had spoken feelingly of the sweet shrub and evening primroses that bloomed in the low places, of the Queen Anne's lace that bloomed along roadsides and filled old fields. It was true she had mentioned nesting quail and the song of the field larks. But proponents of the airport had never stopped kidding her about being an advocate for possums. She had not mentioned possums, having no love for the ones that raided Miss Willie's hen house. But she let it go. Between possums and land spoilers, she would side with the possums.

There was a general stirring of guests leaving the table and Kate decided that she should go and let them map their own strategy. Lucy Aldredge made one more try. "How about the dust? Doesn't it drive you crazy?"

Kate thought of the years painstakingly devoted to planting a thicket to turn back the dust from her cabin. Now Edge, fearless proponent of so-called "progress," installer of floodlights and butcher of sweet-smelling vines, had robbed her of her thicket and these people were doing their best to rob her of her road as well. Fury rose up in her, turning Bets's excellent dinner to boiling rage.

"You all are new here," she said, her voice carrying to the living room, bringing back those who had wandered that far. "You mean well. I'm sure you are good people, but I think you are blind and misguided. You have taken so much, so damned much!" Her voice rose and broke.

She swallowed hard and in a moment she resumed. "This land was loved and taken care of by the Indians. We drove them out. Now we gather their arrowheads and pitiful fragments of pottery and display them proudly as if we had some right to them. Then the cotton planters came in and raped the land with their row crops and turned the streams blood-red with the precious topsoil. Then war—the Civil War—devastated the countryside. You know about that, the destruction of homes and farms, of grist-mills and flour mills and our only local industry, the Roswell Textile Mill. You might say we deserved that, since the sympathy of those of you from up north is bound to be on the other side. But did we deserve the boll weevil? I don't know. I do know that people who could afford to left their plows in the field and moved away and the poor abandoned tenant farmers began to starve. I've seen their scrawny, hookwormy children."

She paused, remembering a little girl in a chicken-feed-sack dress, which her mother had hopefully, ludicrously, tried to improve by whipping a taffeta ruffle around it. The little girl was eating her lunch at a little one-room school down the road when Kate had visited there with a social worker. Her lunch was a single big doughy biscuit lathered with hog lard.

"Her folks grew cotton," the social worker had explained. "They don't know how to raise vegetables and cows and chickens."

The room was now quiet and Kate on impulse related the story she had never been able to forget. The child in her pitiful dress with her greasy biscuit.

"Her folks didn't know how to raise anything but cotton—cotton for somebody else," she said. "But they learned. Small farmers hung on. The earth came back. The depleted fields grew timber. The deep green wood lands gradually returned. The streams ran clear again.

North Fulton County was a place of beauty and peace."

Kate paused and took a deep breath. "And then—and then you all came! Subdivisions, power saws, bulldozers, concrete! Oh, I know you paid the people whose cornfields you took. I know old settlers took your money only to see their old houses bulldozed down or burned. You have built beautiful homes and acquired instant landscaping.

"The only thing you haven't taken is one little country road. Three poor little country miles winding through the woods. Not much left there except memories—Indians drew water from the springs beside it, oxcarts traveled over it, and Revolutionary War and Civil War soldiers passed that way on their way home. Why do you want to destroy it? Why?"

The people in the room were silent.

"Well, I've had my say," Kate said, turning to the door and then suddenly turning back. "And I'll see you in hell before I let you destroy it!"

Edge had put the drunken Bambi in the car and she was sound asleep. He got in the driver's seat and wanted to talk about the road. "I don't see why. . . ." he began. "After all, you can't fight progress."

The hell you can't, thought Kate, but she said nothing except, "I believe I'll walk, Edge. See you at the house."

Walking through what was left of the woods and crossing the little road made Kate sad. A thin crescent moon was bright in the sky and she decided she would go a bit farther down all that remained of the unpaved, undeveloped thoroughfare left to her.

Development had stopped a quarter of a mile away, and beyond that were pastures, old fields, and wooded hills. If she walked to the crooked pine, she would have gone a mile, and she needed that after Bets's dinner. She and Benjy had recognized that the old pine had probably been bent in a bow shape by children riding it when it was a sapling. It was one of her and Benjy's favorite markers for their walk—a mile to the pine, a mile back, good enough for a busy morning.

Beyond the pine the road dropped steeply to a little creek where there was a stand of pink thistles, black-eyed Susans, and, coming on for the fall, the stately Joe Pye weed. When Pepper walked with her, he always plunged into the creek for a swim. Sometimes when Kate had a problem gnawing at her, she would sit on the splintery floor of the bridge and dip her feet into the cold water. The bridge was old and ramshackle and Kate imagined that before the first Model-T hit Loblolly Road the farmers in the area had been glad of the creek. It allowed their horses and mules to stop and drink. *Nobody's got a right,* Kate fumed, *to replace it with a concrete bridge.*

A cloud had obscured the young moon by the time Kate got back up the road to her dooryard and she was startled when a dark figure loomed on the path to the subdivision.

"Who's there?" she quavered, and then to herself, *Dear God, don't let it be a homicidal road paver.*

"It's me, Kate. Bets."

"Well, hi," said Kate. "Is the party over?"

Bet sighed. "Except the dregs. Bob and his lawyer."

"Well, come on in the house and I'll make you a cup of coffee."

"Don't need any more coffee tonight. Can we just stay out here for a minute and talk?"

"Sure," said Kate. "Want to sit here or go in the yard?"

"Your houseguests might hear us if we sit in the yard," said Bets. "This is private." She looked around.

"That bank," said Kate. "It'll stain your pants with red clay, but it is a good sitting place. A hundred years ago, I've heard, the man who lived in my cabin used to sit there with his shotgun waiting for revenuers. When they showed up, he fired off his gun so the neighbors over on the creek making a run of moonshine could make their getaway."

Bets let out a forlorn half laugh.

"You like that old stuff, don't you?"

"Until something better comes along. What's the new word from Shining Waters?" Kate asked as they sat down.

"I'm divorcing Bob."

"What, after tonight's nice party?"

"That was the reason I decided to have a party—a kind of last hurrah. Bob likes it when I bring out the best dishes and put on the dog. Since I'm leaving him and selling the house, I decided on the gesture."

"Oh, Bets, I'm sorry," said Kate, reaching for her neighbor's hand. "Is it absolutely necessary—a done deed?"

"I'm afraid so. I got the papers started yesterday." She was silent a moment and Kate realized that the plain, thin-faced woman was crying. She was glad she couldn't see the tears in the darkness. Bets would hate that.

"I wanted to tell you," Bets said after a moment. "We haven't got very chummy, but I always admired what you wrote and I liked knowing you were here."

"Can't you keep the house and stay? Maybe that's not very practical—such a big house—but I wish you could."

"Bob wants the house—would you believe it? I think

his girlfriend would like to have it. But it's in my name."

"Girlfriend! Is that the trouble?"

"Of course it is." Bets blew her nose, stirred restlessly on the clay bank, and laughed shortly. "I wouldn't leave him otherwise. He wants me to. You know, I love him. I knew he was working late a lot and taking a good many business trips, but I didn't think it was another woman. He finally told me."

Kate sighed. The pain human beings inflict on one another was incomprehensible. *Love, highly touted in prose and poetry and especially in song, is a very perishable commodity,* she thought.

"Do you know who this woman is?"

"I haven't any idea. I know she's a brunette. Hair on his jacket. And her lipstick . . . You think I'm snooping?"

"Of course you are," said Kate. "You have a right. She smears up his shirt, I suppose?"

"Um, very bright. Indelible. Impossible to wash out."

"Oh, Bets, I'm so sorry!"

Bets stood up. "I'd better be off. The real estate people are coming tomorrow. I have to sign a contract with them. I'll see you before I go."

"Where will you go? Have you picked a place to live?"

"I have a sister in California. I'll start there."

Kate walked along the woods path with her and hugged her at the edge of the subdivision. "Let me know if I can help," Kate said before she turned toward her own house.

Bets Dunn's body was found facedown in the Shining Waters fountain by a delivery man the next morning. He was a cousin of the Gandys and, getting no answer when he knocked on the doors of several subdivision houses, he went down to the crossroads to the home of his kinfolks to use the telephone.

Kim Sue and Sheena had spread the word. Their first stop was Kate's cabin.

"Miss Kate, Miss Kate!" the Gandys hailed as Kate sat in the backyard drinking her first cup of coffee. "Another dead body! Miz Dunn over yonder in the pink house is dead. Drownded, our cousin said!"

Kate stood up. "Bets Dunn? Oh, children, how awful! How do you know?"

"Our mommer's first cousin, Lowell, Jr., come to our house to call to law! You better hurry if you want to get there first."

I don't want to get there first, Kate demurred. Perhaps she should have known Bets was suicidal. She should have stayed with her. She supposed she should go and see Bob, but she had no taste for it.

"They're gethering!" proclaimed Sheena. "Them subdivision people is gethering. You hear them?"

Kate hadn't heard them, but, listening now, she did hear voices coming from across the road and through the woods. In a matter of minutes she heard a siren and she knew the police had arrived.

"I don't think I'll go, girls," Kate said. "I believe I'll go on to work and check with the police later. You all go on home."

"Aw, Miss Kate," said Sheena, gravely disappointed. "We want to go over yonder!"

"No," said Kate firmly. "It's no place for children. It's a very sad thing and I won't have people thinking my girls are curiosity-seekers."

"We are," put in Kim Sue unnecessarily.

"No, you aren't," said Kate. "You're nice considerate girls and you don't poke into other people's affairs.

"Now run on home," she directed. "I have to get dressed for work."

She tiptoed into the house quietly, not so much out of concern for her sleeping guests but because she didn't want to have to engage in conversation with them. She washed her face and brushed her teeth at the kitchen sink and then she eased into the closet under the stairs where she had been keeping her clothes since the advent of the Greens.

She had put on clean underwear and slipped into a striped cotton shirtmaker dress when she heard Bambi crying upstairs.

Suddenly the voice lifted in a high childish keen. "I hate this sorry place! I want to go somewhere else! Can't we get out of here?"

Edge made soothing sounds and Shawn on the roll-away bed in the living room lay wide-eyed and very still.

"It's a hellhole!" cried Bambi. "And she's a snobbish bitch! Her dirt road and bushes!"

Who, me? Kate wondered if she were guilty of a reverse form of snobbery—for dirt roads and bushes. She heard Edge say softly, "I know, I know, little darling. I'm gon' try to make arrangements for us to go right away."

Little darling, Kate thought, moving into the kitchen without looking at Shawn. It was enough to make even a little kid sick at his stomach. But the good news was what Edge said about "arrangements." Could he do it? Would they really go—ever?

The Gandy sisters and Miss Willie were in the yard

when she went outside. Kate thought Miss Willie must have heard about Bets and come because of that excitement in the settlement, but the old woman passed over that for another upset.

"Mr. Renty's gone," she said. "Took off in the night. Him hardly able to walk and Kate, he's gone!"

"Can we go a-looking, Miss Kate?" demanded Sheena.

Kate shook her head at Sheena and smiled comfortingly at Miss Willie. "Don't worry. You have done wonderfully to help him. You know it's his nature to ramble and if he wants to do that, we can't stop him."

"You're wise," Miss Willie said, mollified. "I did fix him a good supper and give him my best goosefeather piller for his bed. He knowed he was welcome."

"I'm sure he did," said Kate. "Did you look at the crowd over by the fountain? Maybe he was over there."

"He warn't," said Miss Willie. "I looked over them vultures. That pore woman."

"Miss Willie, ain't suicide the unpardonable sin?" put in Kim Sue. "Like it says in the Bible. There's a unpardonable sin."

"We don't know, young'un," Miss Willie said, turning to go. "What's in the mind of the Lord ain't always for us to know. He might a knowed that lady was a-suffering bad and pardoned her."

Kate stopped by the obit desk when she got to the office. The paper was usually reticent about suicides unless the person was prominent. But she thought she should tell the obit editor, Wally Thomas, to be alert for a report on Elizabeth Dunn's drowning. She and Wally had a private joke about how Kate was always dropping by with stories about people who had died. They were usually the relatives of old friends, who thought they might be overlooked unless some old-timer like Kate realized that they were newsworthy. From her earliest cub days Kate had known that death was important—more important than fires and floods and wars to the families of those it happened to—and she was careful to notify the obit editor to look out for such notices, if she did not write the story herself. Wally called her the "assistant dead editor."

Today he had already heard about Bets Dunn's death. Not from the undertaker—there hadn't been time for that—but from somebody in the medical examiner's office.

"You know it wasn't suicide, don't you, Kate?" he asked.

"I didn't know that," said Kate, and waited for Wally to continue.

"Murder. Whammed on the head with something, then put in the water."

Kate stood very still.

"Any arrests?" she said at last.

"Don't think so," said Wally.

"What time did it happen?"

"Sometime before midnight. I don't know for sure."

"I was with her late," Kate said. "She lives across the road from me."

"You're always at the scene, Kate. Makes me uneasy to be around you."

Kate grinned feebly and went into her office.

This was not going to be one of her favorite days. She didn't mind the work. Writing a column or covering a news story was often a pleasure to her. But she deplored the meetings, those at the office and those of several boards and committees she had been persuaded to serve on. And sometimes an office party like the one today for a retiring editorial writer made her very sad. The organized, on-purpose jollity, the hat-passing for the gift, the speeches and the spread of food well-meaning secretaries had either contributed themselves or bought at the deli. There was always picture-taking and because she was an old-timer she found herself trapped before the lens with the guest of honor. The story in the office house organ would have a head that said, "Remembering when . . ." Always inaccurate because sometimes Kate and the guest of honor, as today, had very little in common. Their work had been in different areas, their acquaintance mainly in the elevator or at other retirement parties like this one.

Kate said her thank-yous and Godspeeds as fast as she decently could, accepted a paper napkin that said "Farewell" as a keepsake, and ducked out to the telephone.

The medical examiner, Rayce Spencer, an old friend of many years, responded quickly and concisely. Bets had suffered a blow to the head, which killed her instantly. Bits of bark in her hair suggested that she had been struck with a heavy stick of some kind. She was already dead when she hit the water. Time of death close to eleven P.M.

Somebody must have been waiting for her when we separated at the edge of the subdivision, Kate mused. The area around the little square with the fountain, which was the center of a cul-de-sac, was tastefully but well lit. Kate should have seen somebody.

"Any suspects?" she asked.

"Not that I've heard of," said the ME. "Isn't that your field?"

"Not if I can help it," Kate said. "I just happen to know Mrs. Dunn. Neighbors."

Next she called homicide, where her husband, Benjy, used to be chief of detectives, and got a newcomer, Lieutenant Lester Sumner, who was cautious.

"Gon' call you, Mrs. Mulcay, heard you were the last person to see her alive."

"Who said that, Lieutenant?"

"Can't tell you that." Kate heard him shuffling papers. "A witness. Need to come out to your house for a little talk."

"Sure," said Kate. "I'm still at the office but I should be home in an hour. Have you talked to Mrs. Dunn's husband?"

"Yes. Grief-stricken. He has an alibi. His lawyer was with him. They went into town and had a few drinks at a bar. The bartender and several other people will back him up on that."

Kate didn't believe Bob was grief-stricken, but she made up her mind as she drove up 400 not to say so. He could be fooling around and still care about Bets. He might be caught up in remorse for his infidelity. It wasn't up to her to express an opinion.

But the second thing she said to Les Sumner when he pulled up a chair in the backyard to begin his inquisition of her after "Hello" was, "You knew they were getting a divorce? He had a girlfriend."

"No, I didn't know that," the handsome young detective said. He was young for his responsibility, dark-haired and clean-cut, good-looking as Benjy had been in his early days.

"We have a witness who saw you with Mrs. Dunn very late," he began. "Care to tell me what that was about?"

"That," said Kate. "The divorce. That was about it. The Dunns had a bunch of us over for dinner and after everybody went home Bets came to see me."

"She knocked on your door," prompted Lieutenant Sumner. "Said she wanted to talk and you went outside. Anybody see you?"

"No," said Kate hesitantly, trying to remember. "I was already out in the road. I had gone for a walk after supper and was just coming back. Bets was out there waiting for me."

"She knew you were taking a walk?"

"*No!*" said Kate irritably. "I guess she was coming to see me and we both got there at the end of the path at the same time. Coincidence."

She knew Lieutenant Sumner didn't believe in coincidences. Hardly any law enforcement officer did. And the old taking-a-walk-alone was the oldest of alibis. But it was patently silly that Les Sumner would talk to her as if she were a murder suspect.

"Lieutenant," she said boldly. "Am I a suspect?"

"Aw, now, Mrs. Mulcay," he said, "you know how that is. Everybody has to be questioned. It just happens that you were . . ."

"The last person to see her alive!" supplied Kate. "Well, I can tell you exactly what happened. Bets came to tell me that she was getting a divorce and selling the house and moving. It is in her name. We sat on the bank out there by the road and when she finished telling me that her husband wanted a divorce because he is seeing another woman, she got up to go and I walked with her to the edge of the subdivision. That's all."

"And then?"

"I came home and went to bed."

"Witnesses?"

"I don't think so. I have some houseguests, but they had come in earlier, so I don't imagine they knew when I came in."

"Two things," said Lieutenant Sumner. "Do you often walk down this country road by yourself at night?"

"When I feel like it," said Kate curtly.

"And you happened to feel like it last night?"

"Obviously."

"Why was that?"

"I don't know!" Kate cried irritably. She did know, but she wasn't telling this sleek young officer. She was worried about the paved road discussion. She was surprised that Edge had sided with the opposition when it wasn't any of his business and he was certainly there on her sufferance. And then Bambi . . . if Kate were the type to embarrass easily, she would have been mortified that Bambi was drunk and falling in her plate. "I just felt like it," she said. "But don't you think you should Miranda me?"

"I hadn't thought of it," Lieutenant Sumner said easily. "But there is one thing more. You got in an argument about the road over there, didn't you? You were pretty angry about that?"

"Well!" said Kate, laughing. "At last the motive! I would do in Bets Dunn over paving a dirt road! How do you know she was in favor of it? After all, she was selling out. Besides, there was no argument. I simply disagreed with some people who said it should be paved and that was about it."

The young officer didn't look convinced, but he stood up and put away his notebook and pen. He declined coffee or a soft drink and moved gracefully to his unmarked car and drove off.

Edge and Bambi came out. They had obviously been listening at the kitchen window.

"You heard the news?" Edge said.

Kate nodded. "The way Lieutenant Sumner questioned me about it, you'd think I was the one who did Bets in."

Bambi, still puffy around the eyes, burst into tears. "She was the sweetest thing!" she cried.

Kate was on the verge of saying *Who?* and caught herself. Of course Bambi would belong to the canonize-the-dead school. Kate had liked her late neighbor, but she hadn't thought of her as particularly sweet. But then, Kate didn't value sweetness in people overly much.

"What did you all do today?" She addressed the question to Edge.

"Not much," he said.

"We didn't have a car!" cried Bambi tearfully.

Edge looked uncomfortable. "We went over to the Dunns and tried to help the police a little. And Bob. We let him know we sympathized and were here if he needed us."

You're here, *all right*, Kate thought, *and I haven't heard any more about those "arrangements."*

Before she could get in the house and change her

clothes and start thinking about supper, the Gandys came bouncing across the road. They had been to the Dunn house, after she forbade it.

They anticipated her accusation.

"We didn't go to the Dunns'," Sheena said hastily. "We been to Miss Willie's looking for Shawn. He wasn't there and Mr. Renty, he ain't came back yet, either."

"He may have done the murder, running off like that," offered Kim Sue thoughtfully.

"Kim Sue, don't say things like that," Kate ordered. "Mr. Renty wouldn't hurt a flea. Besides, he's old and weak."

"Yeah, pore thing," said Sheena. "We oughter go find him."

"Where is Shawn?" Edge asked.

The girls shrugged. They hadn't seen him all day. He was due to be over at Miss Willie's working in his little patch of garden, but they hadn't seen him. They even waded in the creek thinking he might be there.

"I believe I'll walk over that way and see if I can find him," Edge said.

"We'll go with you," volunteered the Gandys.

Thank goodness, thought Kate. She planned to pay a call on Bob Dunn and she didn't need them along. Supplies for supper seemed scarce and she decided to do a daring thing—leave it up to Bambi.

"How about bacon and eggs for supper? Or we could have BLT sandwiches. We still have plenty of tomatoes. What do you think?"

Bambi snuffled miserably. She didn't know, she said.

"Well, you decide," said Kate. "I'm going to run over to the Dunns'. Whatever you come up with will be fine by me."

* * *

Bob Dunn was sitting by the swimming pool with a drink in his hand. Two men friends were with him and several women were busying around in the house. Kate paused only long enough to express her sympathy and ask if there was anything she could do.

"The notice in the paper," Bob said tentatively.

"You know under the circumstances it's a news story. Was there something special you wanted to add to the notice the funeral home gave us?"

He shook his head. "I think I told them everything. Place and date of birth, schools, service with the Roswell Historical Society and the theater group. No relatives except me."

Kate paused. "No relatives? I thought Bets mentioned a sister."

Bob dismissed that with a wave of his hand. "A poor thing. She has Alzheimer's. I don't want to worry her with it even if she had mind enough to understand."

Kate mumbled again that she was sorry and turned to go.

"Kate," Bob called after her, got up and walked toward her. "They told you it was murder, didn't they?"

"Yes," said Kate. "I wasn't going to mention it. I know it must be very painful for you. Do you have any idea who did it?"

"I didn't," he said unexpectedly. "I have witnesses that say I was in town at the time."

"What would make anybody think you would do it?" asked Kate.

"What would make anybody think *you* would do it?" countered Bob.

Kate started to protest and then she thought of Lieutenant Sumner. Maybe somebody did think she did it.

She walked home slowly. She started to sit down under the maple tree, but the kitchen telephone was ringing.

Biddy Stubbs, the feisty little Audrey Hepburn–looking girl who covered police for the paper, was calling.

"Katie, I'm probably not supposed to tell you this," she said breathlessly, "but did you know Beau Sumner thinks you killed that neighbor of yours?"

Kate laughed—but shakily. "Is that what they call him—Beau?"

"Oh, yes!" said Biddy. "He's so adorable. Don't you think?"

"Not if he's going to charge me with murder," Kate said.

"No joke," said Biddy. "He's got you at the head of the list. I saw it on his desk."

"Who else is on there?"

"Oh, a nutsy old man. You can't call him a street person because he lives in the sticks. How about a woods person?"

"Well, for goodness' sake! Beau is bonkers!"

"Just thought I would tell you, cutie," concluded Biddy, who called everybody, including the police chief and the city editor, "cutie."

"Wait a minute, Biddy, do you know what was used to kill Mrs. Dunn?"

"Sure," said Biddy. "An oak tree—or a piece of one. Sapling. Is that what you call it, a little oak tree? Anyhow, they haven't found it yet, but they're pretty sure that's what did it. It had bark on it because that's in her hair and it had to be small enough for somebody like you—or that old man—to swing."

"Hmn, I think I know what did it. Not who, but what."

"Use it for your defense, hon," said Biddy, and hung up.

Kate turned from the phone. Bambi in shorts and pink rayon bedroom scuffs was poking drearily around the kitchen. She had out the eggs and bacon. Kate decided to help her by skinning the tomatoes.

Edge came back in a moment looking discouraged.

"Oh, Lord, you didn't find him!" Bambi cried.

He shook his head and Bambi burst into tears.

"He's gone, he's gone again! That policeman came this morning and scared him! Oh, my baby boy!"

She crumpled into the kitchen rocker and Kate took the eggbeater out of her hands.

"What policeman?" she asked.

"One of them from over at the subdivision. Looking for you. Wanted to know your whereabouts last night."

"You told him I was here?"

Edge looked uneasily at Bambi. "I didn't know. I went right to sleep. Bambi was wakeful and she heard you and Bets having words out there in the road."

"We were talking, just talking," Kate said. "Is that what you call 'having words'? Does Bambi plan on having me charged with murder?"

"Don't, Kate," pleaded Edge. "She didn't mean no harm."

A wave of fresh weeping swept over Bambi as she rushed from the kitchen and headed for the stairs. Kate looked after her with more sympathy than she knew she was capable of. It was so pitiful to be Bambi. In her own home she might not be guilty of such gross ineptitude. Now she was probably hitting the bottle in an effort to ease her pain.

Kate turned to the skillet to check on the bacon and eggs. While they were cooking she set the table for four and, because she needed a lift, she stepped out in the yard and gathered a bouquet of herbs to put in the little yellow McCoy cup for a centerpiece.

Bambi did not return to the kitchen, although Edge went upstairs to try to persuade her. And Shawn did not come.

"Edge," Kate said as they ate together, "why is Shawn so afraid of policemen?"

Edge looked over his shoulder, checking the living room and stairwell. "I'll tell you," he said softly. "I reckon you're entitled to know. A while back when I was still working in the oil fields, Bambi got real drunk one night and got picked up for DUI. They took her to jail and Shawn was in the house by himself all night. He was scared she wouldn't ever come back and he blamed the police. A neighbor wired me and I come straight home, but he never got over it."

"Well, getting drunk and driving . . ." Kate began, but what was the use?

He obviously knew it was scary for a little boy and dangerous for a woman.

"It put a mark on him. He won't ever forget it. She's still drinking and when the police come . . ."

"Have you tried to get help for Bambi's drinking?"

"Sure. A.A. But she won't go. I've tried fussing with her about it, pouring out whiskey, hiding bottles . . . everything."

All Kate could say was "I'm sorry." She was ashamed that she had so little patience with Bambi's alcoholism. She was ashamed that she had been angry at Bambi's expenditures on her credit card—the silly yellow dress with the bow on the behind. How much had it cost? And the money she gave them for groceries and there were few groceries. Did it all go for liquor? She sighed and stood up to clear the table.

Going to jail for murder might be better than this, she thought wryly.

Edge made an ineffectual effort to help her put the dishes in the dishwasher and then went upstairs to Bambi. *He loves her,* Kate thought, *poor fool.*

When the kitchen was neat, Kate wandered out to the yard, half looking for Shawn, half looking for surcease from her worries. What ever happened to the lazy late summer days when she could lie in the hammock and read or prowl over the yard wondering if she had room for a Cherokee rose?

She decided to visit Miss Willie.

Miss Willie was in the kitchen making persimmon bread. The ancient wood range had heated the whole house and the old woman mopped at her face with the tail of her apron.

"Set on the porch, Kate," she directed. "I'll have these loaves out in a minute. I was making them to take to Mr. Dunn."

Aw, funeral meats, thought Kate. She had not thought of it, but she supposed she should make a covered dish or cook a ham or something. It was one of the customs of the country that newcomers and subdivisions had not changed. In time of the heart's pain people did what they could for the body. She would go to the store tomorrow.

Miss Willie came out of the kitchen, the back of her old gray Mother Hubbard dark with sweat and her feet bare.

"Ooh," said Kate enviously. "You're as barefooted as a bird dog."

Miss Willie smiled. "I am a bird dog," she said. "I been tracking them missing ones."

"You knew that Shawn has turned up missing?"

Miss Willie nodded. "He ain't fur. That young'un don't want to leave his garden. Wheresoever he went, he got back here sometime today and watered his patch. He's afraid of near 'bout everything—his ma's condition first of all. And Kate, he don't want to leave here and roam with them like she's a-begging to do."

"How did you know that?" Kate asked.

The wrinkled, sun-browned old face split in a smile. "Don't you know them Gandy girls hear everything and tell most of it?"

Kate grinned ruefully. It was true. Sheena and Kim Sue were the original little pitchers with big ears.

"I'm afraid the Greens are not going anywhere. How can they? No job, no money, no car."

Miss Willie was not one to dwell on an impasse.

"Let's go cool our feet in the creek," she said.

For an hour the two women sat on the creek bank where the moss was like velvet and the ferns grew tall and thick. The water was pure and clear and made a rushing sound as it flowed over a little rock dam the children had made. There were colored pebbles on the sandy bottom near the bank and Kate reached for one with her toes.

"Be careful you don't bring up a spring lizard," Miss Willie joked.

Kate hastily drew up her feet.

Miss Willie laughed. "Ain't gon' hurt if you do and we'll have bait for fishing—if Shawn gits back soon."

Back in the woods a Phoebe bird called its name, a questioning "Sweet Phoebee" over and over again. A hawk circled toward Miss Willie's chicken yard and apparently as a gesture of goodwill circled away and soared high over the hills beyond the river. A Monarch butterfly lit on Miss Willie's bony knee and fluttered its gold and black wings a moment before it flew on.

Both women watched silently.

After a time, Kate said, "You mighty quiet today, Miss Willie."

"Only a fool has a multitude of words," the old woman responded.

"Who you quoting?" Kate asked.

"The Good Book, o' course. Hits the only book we ever had. Cy could read and he read it to me and little Garney every day."

Kate knew Miss Willie still grieved for the stepson she reared and had to be cleared of murdering. She hadn't done it, although he abundantly deserved it. *Maybe I deserve to be blamed for Bets's death. I didn't kill her, but I wasn't glad to see her house go up, nor any of those in back of paved streets and landscaped yards. I should have been more tolerant, more welcoming. It was selfish of me to want to keep Shine Creek the way it was. It would be poetic justice to accuse me of killing one of them when I only* wanted *to kill the developer—and that was a long time ago when I was younger and in love and new to the country and naively believed that nothing would change.*

"It really is the good book, Miss Willie. If you only have one, it should be that one. It puts wonderful words in your mouth and wise thoughts in your head."

Miss Willie seemed to be listening—not to Kate but

to some other sound, rocks and trees and water. She could smell them, she once told Kate, also sunshine and rain and thunder and the days of the week.

Kate believed it and she believed that the old woman's intuitions were better than the newest methods of crime detection.

"Who did it, Miss Willie? Who killed Bets Dunn?"

The old woman shook her head. "Hit ain't the time of day to be shore," she said. "We could be a-looking and a-searching at first light afore folks is stirring?"

It was a question and Kate answered promptly. "I'll meet you here at four o'clock tomorrow morning."

The thick summer darkness had not yet thinned when Kate awakened. And Shawn's young body was not on the rollaway bed. She scrambled into sneakers and jeans and stopped by the kitchen sink to dash cold water onto her face. She longed for a cup of coffee, but Miss Willie would be waiting for her.

Edge and Bambi were quiet, apparently sleeping, and the subdivision, as she cut through it, was sleeping, too. There were lights on in the Dunn house but no sign of life. In the old days, when she and Benjy first came to the country, in time of a death the body would be in the front room and friends and relatives would have sat up with it all night. Now sitting up with the dead seemed to be an empty ceremony. She wondered if somebody found it necessary to sit up with the widower.

Miss Willie had a kerosene lamp burning in the kitchen and she met Kate at the door and motioned her in.

"Coffee's ready," she whispered. "We gon' need it to strengthen us."

"Bless you," said Kate, walking toward the warmth of the kitchen range and the fragrance of coffee dripping into a gray graniteware pot through a white cloth strainer. Miss Willie still roasted green coffee beans and ground them in a little tin grinder nailed to the kitchen wall. Her coffee was dark and heavy and better than any coffee in the world.

Kate drank from a thick crockery cup and watched as Miss Willie tucked some cold biscuits and fried fatback into a striped ticking bag she had made years ago to carry her fishing tackle.

"You taking a picnic?" Kate asked.

"Not for you and me," Miss Willie said. "But if we was to find any strays."

"Oh, I been wondering what Mr. Renty would have to eat, and Shawn . . . I reckon he's hungry, too."

"Best way to bring him home. But the old man, he ain't likely to come back and there ain't much fruit ripe for the taking this time of year."

"I even wondered where you got persimmons for your bread. I can't believe you'd use green ones."

"I had some of last year's put up in a little brown sugar. Just right for the bread. I even had hickory nuts to go with it. Here," she said, giving Kate a slice. "I made a extry loaf for your company. You might as well sample it."

Kate was glad to sample the dark sweet bread with the autumnal taste of what Euell Gibbons called sugar plums. "Let's take it with us," she said. "If we find Shawn, he'll love it."

They were well on their way when Kate remembered her dog Pepper. He always followed her, but she had not seen him since breakfast the day before.

"Likely he's with Shawn," said Miss Willie. "They took to one another right away."

"I'm gon' call him," said Kate. "He always comes when I call him."

As they plunged through the dark woods, she tried again and again, but there was no answering yelp, no scramble through the underbrush.

"Miss Willie, they must be far, far away," she said despairingly.

But the staunch old woman marched ahead, saying nothing.

Streaks of brightness appeared on the eastern sky and a dark-winged bird swooped over the women, so close to their heads Kate felt the rush of wings. She shivered and involuntarily put up her arms for protection.

Miss Willie chuckled. "Just a owl going home to sleep."

Predawn light, gray and misty, swathed the hillside as they reached the Big Rock. Miss Willie held up a hand to halt Kate and knelt on the ground to peer under the shelf of granite. There was a little pile of ashes, the stub end of some half-burned sticks, and one live coal. In the little patch of soft earth there were dog tracks.

"They was here," she whispered, smiling up at Kate.

"But where are they now?" asked Kate distractedly.

Miss Willie stood up and brushed the leaves and moss off the front of her dress.

"Let's try across the river."

They took off their shoes and waded the river. On the other side they took seats on the sand to put them on again.

"We could try the old house," Kate said. "Mr. Renty

might have gone home—and maybe Shawn and Pepper with him."

The sun was well up and gilding the faded skim-milk face of the old house with a rosy glow when they reached the picket fence. Kate missed the lineup of stuffed animals. They had given the place a kind of false cheeriness when she had been there before, better than pink flamingos or little concrete boys fishing. Only the man-sized bear remained by the door.

"Must have been a pretty place when the family was alive and here," she remarked.

"'Twas," said Miss Willie. "Mrs. Renty had a mighty purty flower garden and she raised the stoutest geese in the settlement. Geese is mean and fractious but good company."

There didn't seem to be company of any kind behind the sagging steps and tilted, go-funny roof. The front door stood open and last year's dried leaves drifted across the porch.

Kate knocked tentatively, called out a weak, half-hearted "Hello?" and then exchanged a look with Miss Willie. They went in.

A dusty hall ran the length of the house. Empty rooms opened on each side. The long windows must have been pretty when they were whole and clean. Now panes were missing and a blood-colored film of clay dust curtained those that remained. Spider webs draped the corners of the rooms and a big hornet's nest was suspended from the old ceiling light fixture in what might have been the living room.

"Do you think Charlene could possibly live here now?" Kate whispered.

Miss Willie shrugged. "Let's keep a-looking."

An L-shaped back porch connected more rooms, probably the old kitchen and a dining room, Kate thought from her acquaintance with houses of this vintage. The porch sagged and creaked as they walked along it to the end room, which, surprisingly, had a padlock on a chain on its door. Kate reached for the lock, which was new and shining, cupping her fingers around it. Astonishingly, it opened to her touch.

She and Miss Willie exchanged looks.

"We could see," the old woman said.

"Looks like we were intended to," Kate said, grinning.

Carefully, nervously, she eased the lock off the chain and gave the door a little push.

It opened to a kitchen—a big old-fashioned kitchen with a beautiful blue-enameled wood range dominating it. There were open shelves filled with dishes that appeared to be clean. A long pine table with a bench on one side and cowhide-bottomed chairs on the other centered the room. Behind the stove there was a fireplace, long unused. Above it was a pine mantel holding a clock—a fine old clock, Kate realized, moving closer. It had a mahogany case and probably wooden works, Kate thought excitedly. She had written a story about a traveling clock collection at the High Museum and this one looked museum-quality. Beyond its painted glass she could see a slender pendulum swinging back and forth.

"It ticks, Miss Willie," she said. "Listen!"

She checked her wristwatch and the hands moving along the Roman numerals, which were encircled by a garland of faded pink roses.

"It's keeping time! Look, it says five-thirty—oh, Miss Willie, look!"

"Is that the time on your watch?"

"Yes, but that's not what I'm excited about. See that four? When it's four I's instead of IV—Miss Willie, that means that it's a very old clock!"

The antiquity of the clock was of slight interest to Miss Willie, who had always lived with old things, but the fact that it was ticking interested her. "They ain't been gone long," she observed.

"Oh, it's probably a thirty-hour clock. They could have wound it and taken off for London or Paris."

"That'd be a good thing—if we gon' look anymore."

Kate's eyes were fastened on the porcelain knob of a door leading out of the kitchen.

"See what you mean," said Kate. "Let's take a look!"

The door opened easily to a dim, heavily curtained room that seemed to contain nothing but a bed—a bed that had been occupied but had not been made up. The covers were tousled, the pillows crumpled. A filmy pink garment—probably a nightgown—lay in a heap on the floor.

They backed out of the room and stood looking at one another in wonderment. Who used the bedroom and the kitchen and where were they now? Why was the rest of the house deserted, dilapidated, and left open to intruders like them—and worse?

Puzzled and somewhat discouraged, the two women sat on the front steps.

"It don't look like no home for Eli Renty," Miss Willie remarked tiredly. "Plenty of room, but he sleeps under a rock."

"And Shawn, where do you suppose he sleeps?"

"Under the rock, too," said Miss Willie. "You saw the dog tracks."

They couldn't think where to go next. Kate looked at her watch and thought of the office. Before they started, Miss Willie dipped into her ticking bag and handed out biscuits and fatback. Kate hadn't known she was hungry, but she ate eagerly.

"'Twill strengthen us," she said in mischievous imitation of Miss Willie.

Bets's funeral was held in the chapel of the Roswell Funeral Home, attended by her fellow members from the historical society and a surprising attendance from the new people of the subdivision. Bob sat alone in the pew reserved for the family and Kate wondered if some of the neighbors should not have been beside him.

Finally a couple from Shining Waters did join him—his lawyer and his lawyer's wife. There was no minister and no music. The couple apparently had been asked to do a eulogy and they did it together, taking turns describing Bets's friendliness, her helpfulness, and her winning disposition.

Kate thought the kind words, well meant, were a pallid substitute for the stately service for the dead: "Eternal rest give thy daughter Elizabeth, O Lord; and let perpetual light shine upon her."

Shawn, trailed by Pepper, had come back from his wandering, both of them briar-scratched and dirty and hungry. Edge and Bambi sat with him between them, each of them holding one of his hands, as if they were afraid he would disappear again.

Kate drove them home after the service and kept her car.

Lieutenant Sumner had asked her to "drop by" police headquarters. She knew it was probably more a command than an invitation, but they weren't prepared with any real evidence against her. It was a fishing expedition only, but she knew it was important to respond.

"Beau," as Biddy had called him, was not so handsome in his shirtsleeves with his shining dark hair uncombed and dark circles under his eyes. He had been up all night because of the shooting of a MARTA bus driver and the sight of Kate seemed to distract and annoy him. He had apparently forgotten that he had summoned her.

"Have a seat, Mrs. Mulcay," he said politely enough. "Would you like a cup of coffee?"

"No, thank you," said Kate. She knew about police department coffee. She and Benjy had once joked that it had been dipped out of the Decatur Street sewer. Maybe it had improved with all the new buildings and crime detection aids, but she decided not to risk it.

Kate was relieved that there was no stenographer to take down what she said. It boded for an informal inquiry instead of serious questioning.

"You understand that I have to put you to this inconvenience," Beau said, offering Kate a smile so princely she could understand how he captivated young female police reporters. "You were the last person to see Mrs. Dunn alive."

Kate waited.

"It is well known that you had a grudge against the subdivision people," he went on. "Those of us who have read your columns have followed that."

Kate couldn't help a little surge of pleasure that he had said "those of us who read your column" like he was a reader, which she certainly doubted. She savored that for a moment before she said, "I don't think you have found that I ever had a grudge against subdivision people. I objected to the development of the woods where I live, but the people who moved there? Of course not! The ones I know I like very much and I realize that I was being an old mossback to hope to keep the area unchanged."

"But you did have words with Mrs. Dunn over the paving of a road?"

"I don't think I did," said Kate. "One of her other guests at supper the other night asked me if I would join them in trying to get the county to pave it and I said I would not. I want to keep it the old country road that it has been for more than a hundred years. I guess I might have elaborated on that."

"And when you met Mrs. Dunn on the road later the discussion was continued."

"Oh, for goodness' sake!" cried Kate, getting to her feet. "Bets wanted to tell me that she was putting their house on the market and moving!"

"Could it have been," suggested Lieutenant Sumner smoothly, "that she felt you were making her life in her beautiful home intolerable by insisting on retaining a dusty old road?"

Kate laughed.

"As if I had that power!" she scoffed. "You know the county better than that. They aren't going to pay attention to the objections of one woman living in a falling-down old cabin when millions of dollars of taxpaying housing across the road speaks."

Lieutenant Sumner looked uncertain.

"Your writing . . ." he began.

Kate laughed again. "Read today, if I'm lucky. Forgotten tomorrow."

She turned toward the door.

"Am I your only suspect?" she asked. "And if so, what do you think I used to kill my neighbor? Have you found the well-known blunt instrument?"

Lieutenant Sumner stood up and grinned his endearingly boyish grin. "We're looking."

"I sympathize with you," Kate said flippantly. "Over there in the subdivision the place is so spiffy and well groomed there probably isn't a twig out of place, much less a stick big enough to kill somebody."

Lieutenant Sumner looked only mildly interested and said conversationally, "You know, Mr. Dunn says it is not true that his wife planned to divorce him and sell their house. They were very happy together and there was no thought of separation."

He paused. "As a matter of fact, your cousins appeared to have known them better than you do and they say the Dunns obviously had a very good marriage."

Kate stared at him in astonishment. Before she could recover and think of an answer, the lieutenant covered a yawn with his hand and murmured, "I won't keep you any longer . . . today. Thank you for dropping by."

The Greens were waiting in the yard when Kate drove up. Edge and Bambi had a bright-eyed expectant look about them that Edge quickly explained.

"Your friend Dip called! He thinks he has a sale for our car—somebody who will pay seventy-five or a hundred dollars for it!"

"That's fine, I think," said Kate. "Do you want to take my car and go in and see about it?"

Edge and Bambi were eager to. They hurried to get in the car, but Shawn hung back. "I'll stay here," he said.

"Good," said Kate. "Let's sit a minute under the tree. I've had a tiring day and I'm hot. Are you?"

Shawn ducked his head and said nothing.

"Neither yes nor no?" Kate teased him. They walked to the glider swing under the tree.

"No, ma'am," he said.

Kate pushed the ground to set the swing in motion, hoping to stir up a breeze. She felt Shawn's sidelong glance on her face. Something was eating on the boy.

Suddenly he said, "Kin I bring you a glass of ice tea?"

"Why, that will be lovely!" Kate said, surprised and touched. She watched the leggy youngster lope toward the back steps. He stopped there and called back to her, "Want your sneakers, too?"

"You're a genius, Shawn," Kate said, smiling. "Nothing makes a hardworking woman so happy as a cold drink and sneakers on her feet. Thank you!"

He came back after a while with one of her holey, dirty old tennis shoes under each arm and a tall glass of tea balanced precariously on a tray.

A *tray yet?* Kate thought. *I wonder what's up.* Aloud she said, "This is lovely, honey. You should have brought some for yourself."

Shawn gulped and sat down uneasily in the swing beside her. He watched her sip the tea and kick off her pumps, wriggling her toes toward the sneakers, which he had carefully set on the ground beneath her feet.

"Cuz'n Kate," he said haltingly. "I got something to tell you."

"I'm listening," Kate said.

He held out a crumpled dirty envelope.

"I stole this," he said. "It was the day I run away. I saw Miss Bets put some money in it and put it in the mailbox and when she died I thought it would be all right if I had it. It's not, is it?"

"No," said Kate, taking the envelope. It was addressed to someone in Carmel, California, a woman. The address was smudged and dirty and Kate could barely make out the name. "We must return this to Mr. Dunn, I guess. Let me change my clothes and cool off a bit and I'll walk over there with you."

Shawn ducked his head miserably. "Couldn't you just take it to him?"

Kate shook her head. "You're the one who has to do that, since you're the one who took it."

He looked as if he might cry. His dirty young hands were trembling. "I never stole anything before," he mumbled. "I was gon' give it to my dad. I thought it would help them."

"Oh, honey!" cried Kate, reaching to hug him. "I know you had good intentions. You're a good boy. But it just wasn't the right thing to do, now, was it?"

He shook his head and a tear slid down his cheek. "There's no way I can help them and my mom cries a lot. I thought if I left and they had the money they'd go on without me."

"Is it much money? Did you see how much Miss Bets put in the envelope?"

"I think a hundred dollars. I was coming from Miss

Willie's and she stopped me to talk about coming to her party and swimming in the pool and while she was talking I saw her stick the money in a paper and put it in the envelope. I went back and got it before the mailman came."

"Aw, Shawn," murmured Kate. "I'm sorry. You shouldn't have, but we'll try to make it right. Wait for me, I'll be right back."

But when she got in the house and started changing to blue jeans, she kept looking at the envelope on the desk and suddenly she had a change of mind. She would not make Shawn give it to Bob Dunn. Confession and apology were indicated, but she thought of Bob Dunn's offenses against Bets, the calm way he sat by the pool with a drink and accepted her death. She didn't want to entrust something to him that was private and personal to the slain woman.

She looked at the name and address again. The best she could figure, it was to Miss Margaret Lowe or Long or Land. Could it be Bets's sister, the one she had mentioned going to? Bob had said she was in a mental hospital, but there was no mention of an institution of any kind on the envelope.

She called Shawn inside. "I've decided we will go on and mail Miss Bets's letter to the person she wanted to have it," she said. "I think you should write a note and tell her you took it and are sorry and I'll write one and tell her about Miss Bets's death."

The relief on the young face was stunning.

Kate got out two sheets of notepaper and a clean envelope. She dictated and Shawn wrote that he saw the money and was tempted to take it but was now very sorry and wanted to return it. Kate wrote that she was a neighbor of Bets's and regretted having to tell her about Bets's death. Kate would be glad to hear from her—sister or friend? She included her address and telephone numbers, both work and home, copied the half-legible address on the clean envelope, and put the original stained envelope inside it. Kate found a stamp and promised Shawn she would get it in the mail downtown tomorrow. To make sure she wouldn't forget it, she tucked it inside her handbag.

Edge and Bambi came back looking crestfallen and glum. The prospective buyer of the car was a kid who had only $25 to pay down, but he had a job and he would pay the remaining $50 within the month.

"Did you take it?" Kate asked.

Edge sighed heavily. "It was better than nothing. We stopped on the way home and bought some beer and hamburgers—our contribution to supper."

"Magnificent!" said Kate cheerfully. "You shouldn't have spent all your worldly goods, but it's great not having to cook in this heat. Let's feast out here at the picnic table."

She glanced at her car and saw it was jammed with hanging bags, boxes and plastic bags, and some clothing that flowed loose and unattached over everything.

Edge saw her look and said, "We got our stuff out of the car." He paused and looked more cheerful. "I got my tools, so I can do some things around here."

Oh, lordy, Kate thought desperately, *now he really will tear up the patch. He will handyman my house and yard out of all recognition.* Aloud she said, "That was wise.

They'll probably come in very handy when you find a job."

"Edge is not a day laborer," Bambi said petulantly. "He just does that kind of stuff as a hobby."

Both Kate and Edge stood by the car, surveying its load blankly. Finally Edge spoke. "Where you want me to put this stuff, Cuz'n Kate?"

Kate attempted a laugh. "Well, you know how much room we have. Where would you suggest?"

"Bambi will want her stuff in our room, I reckon. I can put my tools in the smokehouse. The rest of the stuff . . ."

Kate thought of Morgan Falls Landfill, but instead she said, "Miss Willie's barn is a good dry place. What about storing it over there? We could walk over and ask her after supper."

Edge looked relieved. Bambi opened a beer and found a seat under the maple tree and said nothing.

Shawn drew close to Kate and said eagerly, "I could go ask her. You want me to run over there now?"

Since his abortive attempt to run away, his parents had forbidden Shawn to wander from the cabin with the Gandy girls or over to Miss Willie's. But typically lackadaisical, they forgot to enforce it and presently he resumed his little absences, the happy errands of gardening with Miss Willie and wading and building dams in the creek with Sheena and Kim Sue. He ran now to cinch the barn for his parents' storage.

Kate watched him go. His skinny legs were getting brown.

Miss Willie's barn, long since empty of farm animals and the hay to feed them, was available, and after they had eaten the hamburgers and depleted the six-pack of beer, Edge and Bambi took Kate's car with its load of their possessions around the rutted disused wagon road to the old Wilcox place. They did not ask Kate to go with them and she was glad. Watching them go with Shawn perched on top of a collection of plastic bags in the backseat, she had a forlorn wish that they themselves could be stowed in Miss Willie's barn. She did not claim to be an impeccable housekeeper, but Bambi's nail polish and used Kleenex on the windowsill by the chair where she sat to drink her coffee and read her favorite Bates Bible in the morning somehow offended her. It was a small thing, but at that moment she was happily unaware of a bigger and more distressing evidence of their presence.

That came later.

With the Greens out of the house for a while, she felt free to take a leisurely bath. Enveloped in her terry cloth robe, she headed for the still-sunny front stoop to dry her freshly washed hair.

The front entrance to the cabin, seldom used, had been one of her and Benjy's favorite creations. They had combed the countryside for suitable rocks to build a stoop—a rough structure endlessly beautiful and interesting to them. A flat sheet of flagstone topped it and led from the steps to the front door, but along the sides they had carefully fitted rough chunks of granite and sandstone. Many of these delighted Kate with mirrorlike slivers of mica that caught the light. There were holes between the rocks and it took Kate a long time to decide how to fill them. The solution came from a country neighbor whose old well coping had crevices filled with moss and creeping herbs. Thyme, she had decided, and immediately went to the store for seeds. Little flats of dirt planted with thyme filled the windows of the cabin one winter and when the tiny sprouts appeared, Kate began the task of preparing the rocky bed by hauling dirt from the garden and compost pile and jabbing it into the cracks. It was discouraging work because some of the holes between the rocks were deep and she had lost a lot of the good earth to subterranean passages under the stoop. But by the time the tiny plants were strong enough and big enough to transplant, she had their bed ready.

The thyme had, as Miss Willie assured her, "taken a-holt." Green mounds of the little herb filled apertures between the rocks and led the way to the front door, which was seldom used because, parking in back of the house, it was easier to enter through the kitchen. But when she had time, Kate liked to sit in the sun on the top step and enjoy the diminutive, subtly fragrant garden.

Now, with a towel around her head, she sought that perch.

The thyme was gone.

The rocks were gone—under a layer of cement!

Cement covered the entire stoop, filling every crack, coating every rough mica-laced surface! Her carefully nurtured little mounds of thyme lay on the ground, bare-rooted, limp, and lifeless in the heat.

And to add insult to injury, the Greens—father, mother, and son—had carefully embedded their own footprints in the wet cement and added the date!

"Grauman's Chinese Theater!" Kate moaned aloud, caught between rage and hysterical laughter at the absurdity of it. She started to slump down on the stoop and give way to the luxury of tears but realized she couldn't. The cement was still wet and she would be leaving the imprint of her fanny beside those atrocious footprints.

The best she could do was go out the back door and come around and pick up the desiccated thyme and try to revive it with potting soil and water. She was thus engaged when the Greens came back.

"Oh, you saw how we fixed that pile of rocks at the front door!" said Edge happily.

It's now, said Kate to herself, *now. I have to tell them. I can't put up with them for another minute.* But she saw Shawn's eyes on the pot of limp thyme.

"Them wasn't weeds, was they, Cuz'n Kate?" he asked anxiously.

"No," said Kate. "Thyme. But it's all right."

"Your thyme is my thyme!" sang Edge, and then heartily, "Them cracks in them rocks was bad to catch a woman's heels. Bambi tried walking across that stoop and I saw how it was. Some lady might catch her heel and fall off them rocks. I found your ready-mixed cement in the corn crib. And it wasn't a bit of trouble to pull out the weeds and smooth it over."

He waited for thanks and she saw from his face that Shawn waited, too. He must have helped. She choked at the idea, but she thanked them. If they ever left, she might hire somebody with a jackhammer to come and remove the cement. Meanwhile, she looked at the limp little plants she had raised from seed.

"Would you like to have this thyme to put in your garden?" she asked Shawn. "It's a nice herb to cook with and it smells . . ." She couldn't go on. She couldn't think why it seemed so desirable to her.

"Yes, ma'am," said Shawn. "Git it in the ground and it'll probably come back to life."

* * *

The Greens, still wealthy from the residue of the $25 payment on their car, drove into Roswell to see a movie. Kate walked across the yard, trying to enjoy the twilight, but her mind kept shearing off into the morass of missing and murdered neighbors. Where was Mr. Renty? Who killed Bets Dunn—and why? And inevitably she came back to the Greens and their prolonged visit. Would she ever have her house to herself again, or would she be forever subject to their well-meaning but simpleminded depredations?

The old cypress swing behind the weedy nonproducing garden patch had been a favorite spot for Kate and Benjy to sit in the cool of the evening and wait for moonrise. In those days she had a green growing garden with plants that needed watering, and part of the pleasure of sitting back there was to enjoy the coolness of the wet earth and the fragrance of the freshly washed leaves of the vegetables. Now the hard, weedy earth depressed her and there was really nothing left to water except the tomato plants and the mint bed, which didn't seem to need it anyhow.

She might as well be in the house at her desk, struggling with a magazine piece she had promised to an editor friend. She stood up and put out a hand to stop the swaying swing with its rusty creaking chains. It was an old superstition from her childhood—an empty swaying swing or an empty rocking chair left rocking meant sudden death. Dumb, she knew. Benjy had often laughed at her. But it was her only superstition and she hadn't been able to relinquish it. She was steadying the swing when she heard a rustle in the woods behind her. Not Pepper. He had gone to Miss Willie's and had not yet returned.

Not Sugar, the cat. He was a footpad, a silent traveler. She peered into the shadowy trees.

A man was coming toward her.

"Who's there?" she called out, half ready to turn and run for the cabin.

A young male voice answered—softly. "Theron. Hit's Theron."

Who's Theron? Kate wondered, her mind quickly racing over a list of paroled convicts, the ones her newspaper friends called "Mother Kate's chickens." Then she remembered. One of the kids who had helped her with Mr. Renty.

"Theron!" she called. "I'm glad to see you! What you doing back there in the bushes?"

The blond kid emerged from the woods. "I'm looking for that feller staying at your house sold me the car."

"Oh, that's Edge—Edge Green," Kate said. "He's not here right now. Gone to Roswell to a movie. Is the car running all right?"

"'Taint running," the boy said bitterly. "That car's shit. I want my money back!"

"Aw," said Kate sympathetically. "I'm sorry." She didn't want to say that Edge wouldn't have the money to give back and suddenly she realized she didn't have it either. She could write a check, but she was tired, depressed, and broke, hungry for a decent meal and her own bed to sleep in, and besides, she didn't want to. She simply didn't want to finance Edge anymore.

The kid was dirty and disconsolate and she felt a surge of compassion for him. He was suffering from his association with the Greens, too. She smiled at him.

"Come on up to the house and I'll give you a Coke or something."

"You got a beer?"

She shook her head. "Sorry. Anyway, Theron, you're not old enough for alcohol, are you?"

"I reckon so. I hepped my old man make it in the river swamp till he died of TB. He didn't care if I drunk it, even when I wasn't nothing but a baby."

Kate couldn't fault his family for that. She had heard plenty of stories of poor folks and hard times. And she thought of Elinor Wylie's poem "Let No Charitable Hope": "I live by squeezing from a stone the little nourishment I get." This boy with hair the color of new-cut pine had lived his young life on a rocky ledge where there was not much but stones.

She pushed a kitchen chair toward him and got him a Coke and herself a glass of tea.

"Have you seen anything of our friend Mr. Renty?" she asked.

Theron bobbed his head and swallowed half his Coke at one gulp. "He come by our house and Mommer took him fishing. Caught some, too. She cooked them for him."

"Is he there now?"

"Naw, he don't stay nowhere."

"Well, I worry about him."

"No need to. Mommer has knowed him all her life and she says he's the richest man in north Fulton and Cherokee county."

"Wha-at?" gasped Kate.

"Well, you know he owns a heap of land up here—nearbout all that around that old house of their'n. If I remember right, he owns a lot on this side of the river, too, even them woods around the Big Rock. Mommer says hundreds of acres."

"Gracious," murmured Kate. "That's all stuff the subdivisions would be glad to buy."

"Damn right," said Theron. And then, "Excuse the expression. I'm sorry, ma'am."

Kate smiled to let him know she could take a "damn" now and then and that she appreciated his apology. He really was an appealing kid and she would forever thank him and his friend Clarence for helping her get Mr. Renty out of the woods and to the hospital.

"What does Mr. Renty say about selling some of his land?" she asked.

Theron shrugged. "I don't reckon he knows anything about it. That old man ain't a owner. Mommer says the only thing she ever saw him take possession of was that crazy Braves tie he wears. He's plumb foolish over that."

And my yellow bowl, Kate thought.

"Where's your friend Clarence tonight?" she asked.

"Left him trying to start that no-good car," Theron said. "He thinks he can start any car in the world, but I didn't tell him the camshaft fell out when we turned off the hard road up yonder."

"That's bad, huh?"

"The end." Theron pronounced the death sentence. "That's how come I'm here to git my money back. Man sell you a car with a camshaft cutting loose like that . . ."

"Oh, I'm sure Edge didn't know it. He's an honest man. I think he just doesn't know much about cars."

"Well, as long as he gives me my money back," said Theron.

Pepper had returned and was barking at somebody in the yard. Quickly, before Edge and Bambi could hear her, if they were the ones Pepper was barking at, Kate said,

"Theron, does your mother know who hurt Mr. Renty?"

"I know myself," Theron said in a low tone, ducking his head. "I know all about the whole whopping mess."

Kate had to know, but she heard footsteps approaching the cabin in the darkness. She whispered urgently, "You mean you know who did the murder, too?"

"I know who done it and why," the boy said. "But I ain't telling you, Miss Kate, 'cause I ain't a-wanting to see you kilt."

It seemed far-fetched to Kate, but before she could argue, she went to the door to turn on the yard light. The approaching footsteps receded. There was no one there.

"How funny," she mused aloud. "I'm sure I heard somebody. Could somebody have overheard . . . ?"

"I'm gon' see," said Theron, leaping to his feet and running out the door. Kate heard him pounding across the yard.

In a few minutes he came back. "Whoever it was got away," he said.

They stood together puzzling over it. The Greens weren't back. The houses in the subdivision, swathed in the brightness of streetlights, showed no activity and few indoor lights except for the blue glimmer of television sets here and there. Could it have been Mr. Renty?

"Theron, if it was Mr. Renty he would have spoken to us, wouldn't he? He's shy and funny, but not with you and me."

The boy shook his head. "I better go," he said. "I got to see what Clarence is doing with that old piece of junk. It's mighty nigh sticking out in the road by the borry pit. Somebody might not see it in the dark and could hit it."

"Well, I'll tell Edge you want your money back." And

then, because she didn't want the boy to be disappointed, she did what she had vowed not to do. She mixed in it. "I'm afraid he has already spent it, but Theron, if you really need it, I could give it to you."

"It ain't what I need," said the boy with a flash of pride. "It's what's entitled."

"Of course," murmured Kate, watching him stride down the driveway.

From the road side somebody was approaching. Kate turned and waited until the person walked into the light. It was Bob Dunn.

"Good evening, Kate," he said formally.

"Oh, hello, Bob," Kate responded. "How are you tonight?"

He shrugged. Suitably it should have been a shrug of sadness and uncertainty, but Kate, looking at the handsome face in the too-bright yard light, had a feeling that Bob Dunn felt somehow cheerful and even a sort of excitement.

"Won't you come in?" she asked. "I doubt if I have a drink to offer you, but there's coffee and tea."

"Oh, no, thank you," he said. "I must be on my way. I wanted to tell you in case any of your law enforcement pals ask. And also"—he glanced over his shoulder toward the subdivision—"in case burglars or fire or some other disaster strikes my house, I'm taking a trip."

"Oh, somewhere special?"

"I don't know yet. I just need to get away. I plan to just get in the car and drive. It doesn't much matter where I end up."

Now there was a suggestion of sadness in his face and the droop of his broad shoulders.

"Sometimes that's the best way," Kate offered. "I'll keep an eye on your house. Is there anything else I can do?"

He shook his head and turned away. He was at the edge of the yard when Kate thought to call after him. "Bob, were you over here earlier? Just a few minutes ago?"

He half turned before he answered. And then he said shortly, "No, of course not!"

Well, don't get mad about it, jerk, Kate thought but didn't say.

She went inside to her desk and shuffled notes around for a little while but had not even made a start on the magazine piece when the Greens returned. One who prided herself that, having been reared in the newsroom, she could work anywhere under any circumstances, she was dismayed to find that she simply couldn't get syllable to paper with the Greens in the house. It wasn't that they talked to her, although they did some of that. It was simply that they were a disturbing presence. She turned from her desk and put down her lap computer.

"Did you happen to meet Theron, the boy who bought your car, on the road?" she asked.

"Nope," said Edge. "How was the car running?"

"I believe he said it quit on him. Something about a camshaft."

"Good God a'mighty," muttered Edge to himself, not looking at Bambi, who teetered woozily toward the stairs.

High heels for a neighborhood movie, Kate thought wonderingly, and then, looking at the fatuous smile on the plump face, realized that they hadn't gone to a movie at all. They went someplace where Bambi could get drunk.

"Did you enjoy the movie?" she asked with what she recognized was a touch of malice.

"Um-huh," said Bambi, smiling smugly.

Edge looked uncomfortable and gave her a little push toward the stairs. "Come on, baby-child, beddy, beddy."

Shawn came in from a back-porch reunion with Pepper, smiling happily.

"Cuz'n Kate, you shoulda went with me. That was the best movie! Mom and Dad didn't want to see it, so I went by myself. You'd a loved it."

Kate started to invite him to tell her about it, but she heard a siren screaming closer and closer on the paved road and then veering south. The "borry" pit, she thought suddenly. A gravel road led to the old excavation where the county had borrowed clay and fill dirt years ago for the paved road.

"I've got to go!" she cried to Shawn. "Tell your parents." *The keys better be in the car,* she added to herself. Edge was prone to put them in his pocket, despite Kate's repeated insistence that nobody stole cars in that area and she needed the keys where she could find them. For a wonder, they were in the ignition.

She raced the motor and screeched out of the driveway. *Trouble, trouble,* she thought in a desperate premonition.

A small group had gathered at the edge of the old clay pit and two uniformed people, a man and a young woman, were lifting a stretcher into the ambulance.

"The car's down there," said a man who lived at the end of the gravel road, aiming his flashlight at the pit. Its bottom had filled with so much muddy water that only the rusty top of Edge's old car showed.

"Was he in it?" Kate asked, looking at the sheeted body on the stretcher.

"Not that one," said the neighbor. "He was laying here in the road when I got here. I think the other one is over there. The one on the road . . ." He cleared his throat. "All smashed up. Dead."

Kate walked to the edge of the pit where a young man sat hunched over, with his hands covering his face and his shoulders shaking in a paroxysm of weeping.

"Clarence?" Kate said tentatively, unsure in the dim light of her flashlight.

"Ma'am?" answered the boy, turning toward her a dirty face with tears streaming into his pitiful little ambitious, teenage beard. It was Clarence.

She sat down on the ground beside him and put an arm around his shoulder. "I'm so sorry. It's Theron, isn't it? I just saw him about an hour ago. What happened?"

The boy she had thought was a reckless marijuana-smoking young criminal clung to her hand with one of his greasy young paws. His eyes and nose were streaming and he swiped at his face with his sleeve until Kate pulled out a handkerchief from her jeans pocket and thrust it into his hand. The story came out.

Theron, disappointed at not getting his $25 back from Edge, had decided to try to get the car going himself. He had the camshaft in his hands and had crawled under the car to see if he could fit it back.

"Thang was just hanging here on the edge of the borry pit," Clarence went on. "I was afeared it would roll and I walked over yonder in the woods to git a rock to put under the wheel. I got it and was coming back when this car come racing down the gravel and plowed straight into Theron's car. It went in the pit and the son-of-a-bitch backed up and run over Theron and run over him again and him—" his voice broke and he sobbed out the rest, "him just a laying there helpless. Helpless, Miss Kate!"

Kate found she was crying herself.

The police came and threw floodlights over the terrain and sent a man down to check the half-submerged car for more bodies. Finding none, they decided to leave the car till morning when they could get a road machine to haul it out. A young officer got Clarence to repeat his story and asked for details about the assaulting car and driver, none of which the boy seemed able to supply.

"I know you're upset," the officer finally said. "I think it would be a good idea for you to ride into the station with me and let me get your statement in writing."

The boy looked terrified.

"How old are you, Clarence?" Kate asked.

"Seventeen," he mumbled.

"Don't you think you'd better notify his parents?" Kate asked the policeman.

Before the policeman could answer, Clarence shook his head. "Dead," he said. "Theron's the only family I got."

"You got me," Kate said firmly. "I'm going with you."

The policeman looked surprised, but he made no objection, and when Kate insisted on taking Clarence in her car, he agreed. He did not know Kate, but he apparently assumed that at her age she would not attempt to take the kid on the lam. At least she looked clean and respectable and had gray in her hair. Depressing to her, but sometimes useful.

They waited in a little room at the Morgan Falls county annex and Clarence, who had apparently been there before, was now too tense for tears.

"What they gon' do, Miss Kate?" he asked fearfully.

"Oh, nothing to you," Kate said more easily than she felt. "They just want to find out all they can about the car that hit Theron. Did you see it?"

"Just from a distance across the borry pit. Its lights was in my eyes and I saw what it done—but that's all."

"I always thought boys your age could tell the make and year of a car by hearing the sound of its engine in passing," Kate remarked conversationally.

Clarence shook his head. "Not evva time."

He knows, Kate thought. *He did recognize that car.*

The officer came back with a stenographer. The story Clarence repeated was the same one that he had told Kate beside the borrow pit. From a card in the wallet on Theron's body the officer had learned the whereabouts of his mother and sent somebody to notify her.

"Now give me *your* address and telephone number," he said to Clarence.

"Same as Theron," the boy said, his voice breaking. "I been a-staying with them down there on the river. They ain't got a phone right now."

Kate knew the term "right now" was a prideful way of suggesting that they could have a telephone if they wanted but had decided against it.

"How can I get in touch with you?" the policeman asked.

Clarence looked uncertain.

"Call me," said Kate. "Here's my address and phone

number." She handed him a card. "I'll find Clarence for you. We're neighbors."

Clarence looked relieved, as if not having street and telephone numbers might be a hanging offense and Kate had saved him. The policeman was through with them and they stood up to go.

"I can walk back to the house," Clarence offered with country courtesy.

"Oh, no, I'll take you," Kate said. "I want to speak to Theron's mother."

The shack by the river was so rickety it looked as if a light wind might tumble it into the river. It was full of people. Half a dozen men were hunkered down under the riverbank's one big tree, to which the house seemed lashed by ropes. They nodded to Kate and Clarence and went on with a desultory conversation. But inside, a prayer meeting seemed to be in progress. Women of all ages knelt on the floor around the two double beds that filled the room. Their hands were clasped and their heads bowed, while a fat woman backed up to the iron heater in the center of the room whacked on a Bible and exhorted them to prayer.

Clarence backed out and Kate was about to follow him when the woman with the Bible called, "Come in, sister, and pray with us!"

A scrawny woman with a leathery sun-browned face and arms and faded brown hair sat flat on the floor, rocking back and forth in a frenzy of grief. "Lord God, hep us, hep us, hep us!" she moaned.

"Theron's mother?" Kate whispered to Clarence.

"Yes'm," he said. "Miss Arnie's her name."

Kate couldn't refuse to join them. She tiptoed into the room and knelt down at the one space left beside one of the beds. She didn't know how to join the responses of the others when they cried "Yes, Lord!" and "God save us!" It all seemed so sad and shabby and a little sordid to her, this naked emotionalism. But she clasped her hands and closed her eyes and found herself silently praying with the boy's mother, "Hep us, hep us, hep us!" It was too late to help Theron, and what kind of life had he had in this poor little shack? However little he and his mother had, they had apparently been glad to share it with Clarence. It made her ashamed that she was so grudging with her hospitality to the Greens.

The prayer session seemed interminable to Kate, but she didn't want to leave before it was over. She felt an urgent need to talk to Miss Arnie alone and to learn if, as Theron had said, his mother knew everything about Mr. Renty and the death of Bets Dunn. And now, what did she know about the death of her own?

But it was not to be.

The crowd of mourners had thinned to two or three who seemed bent on staying the night. Kate followed Miss Arnie to the little lean-to kitchen and whispered that she would like to talk to her privately if possible.

"Not about my boy! He ain't done nothing!" the woman cried.

"No, not just Theron," said Kate. "The other things that have been happening—the bad things. Theron said you know—"

Suddenly the woman toppled over in a faint.

She sprawled on the splintery board floor, her eyes rolled back in her head, her hands clenched convulsively, a thin stream of spittle running out of her mouth.

Before Kate could reach for a dipper of water and kneel beside her to bathe her face, the people in the other room crowded in.

"Lord God, Arnie's having one of her spells!" cried one of the women. "Raise her head! Git her tongue before she swallers it!"

"Here, here's a spoon to put in her mouth!" said another.

Not knowing what to do, Kate backed away so they could get to the woman.

A man who had heard the commotion and come in from the yard summarized the situation. "Just one of her epileptics," he said, and, losing interest, turned away.

Kate waited until Arnie was conscious and had been stretched out on her bed with a damp cloth on her forehead before saying her good-byes to the women in attendance. To Arnie, Kate said she would come back the next day and take her to Atlanta to see her son's body, if she wanted her to.

"She'll be much obliged, I know," the plump leader of the prayer service said. "She ain't got a car and I don't think her son's car is a-running so good."

An understatement if I ever heard one, Kate thought bitterly, but she smiled and nodded her head and made her way over the rickety floor to the door.

The Greens had already gone to bed by the time she drove into her yard, and even if they had been awake they weren't the ones she longed to talk to. She would like to talk to Miss Willie, but the old lady was an early-to-bedder, too, and Kate hesitated to make her way through the subdivision and down the wooded path with everybody presumably on the lookout for murderers. Instead she took a chair in the backyard, eased off the sneakers she had seemingly had on for days, and reviewed all that had happened since she first came home and changed to jeans and sneakers. There was Shawn's purloined $100 she meant to get in the mail. Now, after the death of Theron, she felt things were really piling up on her. She needed to talk to Arnie, but since the epileptic seizure she was afraid to do it alone. Grief and fear from knowing more than was safe for her to know might bring on another seizure and Kate didn't want to see it, much less be responsible for it. And Bob Dunn, where did he go and how much of her and Theron's conversation had he heard before he made an appearance in the backyard? She felt positive that he had been there before.

More than anything, she felt a terrible tiredness and unexpected sense of grief and loss for young Theron. She had only seen him once before, under circumstances that made her certain he and Clarence were preparing to steal the staff car.

But there had been a tenderness in him when they carried little Mr. Renty across the creek. There had been concern. He couldn't have been more than sixteen and he had never had anything except the damned Greens' useless car. Who would destroy a kid like that?

She knew the answer even as she asked herself the question. The same person who killed Bets Dunn.

The loose gravel on the road by the borrow pit did not retain car tracks and her friend Sergeant Corky Corcoran said there were no real clues to identify the death-dealing car. All that was left was to find the driver, and Corky suggested with a faint attempt at humor that that was Kate's department.

"You say that because I'm such a talented sleuth?" Kate suggested into the phone.

"Naw," said Corky, "because Beau thinks you are in this one up to your neck."

"That's preposterous," said Kate. "No motive, no weapon, no opportunity, and no experience with violence."

"Ha!" jeered Corky without rancor. "You been near 'bout done in half a dozen times since I been on the force. You might as well face it, Katie, you attract violence."

"Nuts," said Kate, but even as she hung up the receiver she wondered if it could be true.

The only violence she contemplated now would be against the Greens. They had cooked themselves a bountiful breakfast and left the dishes sitting on the kitchen table. Perhaps because she didn't like eggs herself she had a particular aversion to seeing plates left with the gummy yellow coating of egg yolk hardening on them.

She didn't have to wonder where her houseguests had gone. Shawn was out in the yard with the dog and the cat and Edge and Bambi were giggling and splashing and taking a shower together.

They could have waited until she had dressed and left the house, she thought, but she recognized that the real source of her irritation was that it was sexual play and even if she didn't envy them that—and maybe she did—she had a puritanical conviction that they should have washed their dishes first.

Because of the delay in getting her own lonely shower,

Kate was late getting to the shack on the river to pick up Arnie. The door was pulled to, not locked, but clearly there was nobody at home. She stood a moment on the ramshackle porch, looking down at the river. She saw a line cast into the water from a clump of alders. It didn't seem likely that Arnie would be peaceably fishing while her boy's body lay in the morgue. But then how did the living live, she thought, except by going on with the daily necessity of scrabbling for food and shelter?

She half walked, half slid down the steep bank to the river, and a battered black felt hat emerged from the alder thicket.

"Good morning!" she called, and a man's face and shoulders surfaced.

"Hidy," he said shortly.

"I'm looking for Miss Arnie. Is she about?"

"No'm, she ain't. She had a grievous thing happen to her and she's on her way to the Gradys."

Of course, Kate thought, nodding. *When we Georgians have "grievous" things happen to us, we usually head for old Grady Hospital. There are some heartaches that "the Gradys" can't assuage, but pain and poverty are its standard fare.*

"How did she go? Did somebody pick her up?"

"Not as I know," the fisherman said. "I seen her and Clarence a-walking and I reckon they was on their way to ketch the bus."

"Oh, no!" cried Kate. "That's six miles or more. I was gon' take her."

"Well," said the man, and turned his attention to the cork on the end of his line, which was bobbing. "Atlanta's a fur piece beyond that."

"Atlanta!" cried Kate. "They weren't gon' walk that far!"

"Not if they had the dollar and a quarter for the bus."

Kate didn't wait to debate the possibility of Arnie's not having bus fare. She scrambled up the bank and started her car and backed out of the rocky, rutted yard.

A mile or two down the paved road she saw two people trudging along the weedy footpath. Clarence and Arnie. They walked like plowmen, heads bowed, shoulders hunched, like people who had been a long way and had a long way to go.

She pulled up beside them and opened the door.

"Offer you a ride?"

Clarence looked relieved and glad. The woman stared at Kate shyly, almost fearfully.

"Hit's Miss Kate," Clarence said. "She works in town."

"You be a-goin' to your job?" Arnie asked.

"That's right," Kate said. "It's just a little piece from the Gradys. In fact, I was going there myself."

Kate realized it would be necessary to make sure the ride she was offering was not a favor but something she would be doing anyhow.

The little woman got in the front seat and Clarence, clearly pleased, got in the backseat.

"You know, I offered to take you," Kate said. "I'm glad to have your company."

"Well"—the woman smiled shyly and Kate saw that she was missing several front teeth—"I didn't want to hinder you none."

She eased her feet out of her shoes and Kate saw that they were new patent leather pumps, probably borrowed for this important errand. Her legs were bare, sun-browned and briar-scratched. She would have worn stockings if she'd had them, Kate knew, and suddenly she remembered Theron's $25.

They were halfway to town before she mentioned it. Arnie and Clarence had been so quiet Kate felt reluctant to break the silence. "You know, Arnie," she said boldly, since she herself was too old to call the woman "Miss Arnie," the title servants and mothers' friends gave older women. "My cousin sold that car to Theron and owes him back his twenty-five dollars since the car was faulty."

The woman waited, her gnarled little hands clutching and knotting and unknotting a limp and dingy handkerchief.

"I'll have the money with me when I pick you up at the hospital."

Whatever protest pride was going to pull from her was stopped by Clarence. "That'll be good, Miss Arnie. Hit's a-owing Theron. He would want you to git hit."

Arnie swallowed hard and blinked her lashless eyes to contain the tears that filled them.

"You know that for sure, Clarence?" she asked.

"For sure," the boy said. "He was a-looking for Mr. Green to git hit back just before . . . well, right before the accident."

"'Twarn't no accident," Arnie said. "Hit was a killing."

"Do you know who did it?" Kate asked quickly.

"I got a idy," the woman said.

Kate's impulse was to take her immediately to the police station, but one look at the proud, stiff little back in the faded print dress and the shy grief-stricken face persuaded her to go on to the hospital and the morgue.

Let Arnie do the duty of blood-kin first and she would talk to her later.

Kate knew the business of viewing her son's body and identifying it would not take long, and she decided against leaving them to go to the office. She walked them into the hospital and coped with the information-taker before rushing out to a pay telephone to explain her absence to Shell and to go to the nearest cash machine to get the money she promised Arnie and a little more for groceries at home.

When she got back to the hospital, Clarence and Arnie were standing on the sidewalk so uncertain and anxious-looking she was sorry she had left them. People from her end of the county sometimes lived out their lives and died without ever having been to the capital city only thirty miles away. Sometimes the man of the family walked the then dirt road to Atlanta to the mule market to replace stock to pull his plow. And in an earlier day farmers drove turkeys and pigs to market. But women and children weren't needed for these tasks and therefore seldom made the trip. Kate suspected that Arnie and even Clarence, although born in an age of expressways and fast cars and even public transportation, might really belong to that older time. At any rate, they weren't dissolved in grief and she had expected that.

Perhaps there was something about the chill finality of a slab in the morgue that gave them self-control.

Again they were quiet on the return trip. Kate thought it suitable to ask about funeral arrangements and Arnie said hesitantly, "They said they'd bring me my boy's body."

"Are you going to have him at home?" Kate asked.

"I reckon," Arnie said. "'Taint no place else. We never had no insurance. His daddy's buried at Bright Prospect. I reckon we'll put him there."

"I know that churchyard," Kate offered. "It's a sweet peaceful place. A lot of magnolia trees and pretty headstones."

"Them's nice," said Arnie politely.

"I can hep with the coffin," Clarence offered unexpectedly. "I know where there's some good wide pine boards and I kin git a feller to hep me put 'em together."

Kate kept trying to think how to introduce the subject foremost in her mind. Did Arnie know who killed Theron? But in the sad practicality of funeral arrangements she couldn't bring it up. Poor country people, probably more than rich and stylish city dwellers, valued an elaborate funeral. Arnie would like a satin-lined coffin with silver handles and the obsequious attentions of store-bought undertakers instead of what the neighbors would surely offer. She grieved for her son, but she probably grieved equally that she was unable to "put him away nice." It had probably been the same with her husband, the moonshiner who died of tuberculosis.

Kate was not surprised that neighbors had already assembled at Arnie's house, but she was surprised to see Sheena and Kim Sue there. They rushed to greet her when she pulled into the yard.

"Well, girls, what are you doing here?" she asked as she hugged them.

"Oh, they some of Mommer's kin," Sheena said. "Cousin or something. She sent us to find when the funeral is. She'll be here t'reckly with a chicken pie."

"I reckon the funeral'll be as soon as they git the body," Kim Sue put in. "If they ain't gon' embalm him, he ain't gon' keep."

All-wise children, Kate thought, sighing. They never spared her a graphic detail of the more grisly aspects of life.

"What's your cousin's last name?" she asked suddenly, thinking it was time she found out.

"Arnie?" said Sheena. "Tippens, I reckon. That's what Theron was called when he went to school."

"You mean he hasn't been in school lately?"

"Ah, no," said Sheena, "not after he got to be sixteen year old."

"Tippy, tippy, tippy," sang Kim Sue, mincing toward the steps. "Sounds like a dance."

"Shut up," said Sheena, and they went in the house.

Arnie was surrounded by friends and, Kate supposed, some relatives, although she had seemed to be a lonely person, dependent only on her ability to wrest a living from river and woods. Clarence sat on the edge of the porch, his legs hanging down, and looking desolate.

"Are all these people kin to Miss Arnie?" Kate asked.

Clarence looked vague. "I reckon everybody's kin when hit's a death."

"I reckon," Kate agreed soberly. And then, "Would you ask Miss Arnie to come outside for a minute? I have the money for her and I need to ask her about some things."

"I'll give her the money, but hit's best you don't ask her no questions. She's scairt to talk."

"Why is she scared?" asked Kate. "Nobody's gon' hurt her. If she will tell me what she knows, I'll get the police to protect her."

"Police!" Clarence cried in a louder voice. "You ain't gon' bring no police here!"

The conversation in the room had ceased and everybody turned toward Kate, listening and looking.

Kate lowered her voice. "Two people have been killed and Mr. Renty has disappeared. Don't you know we need police help?"

"They don't hep, they hurt you," Clarence said stubbornly.

Arnie walked out on the porch and touched Clarence on the head. "Say no more, son," she said softly. "Least said—"

"If you gon' say 'quickest mended,'" Kate said crossly, "it's not true. There's bad trouble here somewhere and if we don't bring it out and look at it, no telling how long it will go on or who will get hurt."

"I know you mean well," Arnie said gently, "but let us do it our own way."

"Maybe you're right," said Kate, sighing, "but I don't believe it." She fished the $25 out of her bag and added the $20 she had intended for groceries. "Here's Theron's money," she said, pressing it into the woman's hand.

Arnie turned the folded bills and looked at them. "Ain't that too much?"

"Oh, no," said Kate. "That's what he was due." She started down the rickety steps and turned. "I wanted to buy some flowers for Theron . . . but maybe you'd rather have the money to apply to the funeral expenses?"

"Oh, no!" Arnie said. "Flowers would be nice. Theron would like that the best, wouldn't he, Clarence?"

As soon as she got home, Kate went to the phone and

called a Roswell florist and ordered $30 worth of roses and carnations.

"No bow, huh, Kate?" asked Gerald, her friend at the other end of the line. "I know you hate 'em."

"We-ell, in this case maybe. . . ."

"See what you mean," said Gerald promptly. "Big satin bow. Lavender?"

"Lavender," said Kate.

Once she had watched Gerald making gaudy bows for his flower arrangements and voiced her opinion that they detracted from the flowers.

"Honey, if they ain't got bows, it's a poor funeral," Gerald assured her.

It turned out to be a poor funeral despite the big lavender bow. Theron's body was brought home as soon as the medical examiner had finished with it that afternoon, and before dark, Clarence and some of the men from the area had dug a grave in Bright Prospect churchyard. The fat woman who had led the prayers at the house turned out to be a Holiness preacher and she had conducted the service as the sun was setting.

"It was plumb spooky," Kim Sue assured Kate. "Some of the folks cried, but wasn't no jumpin'."

"Thank goodness," said Kate. She had heard that a proper funeral in the old days had always included a widow or somebody "well kin" who had to be restrained from jumping into the open grave.

"I'm sorry I didn't know," Kate added. "I would have gone."

"Miss Willie, too," said Shawn, who was on the edge of the conversation. "Me and her walked all the way down there to take a cake and wasn't anybody at home. They musta been at the funeral."

"That's it," said Sheena. "All of us went, but wasn't what you'd call a crowd."

Kate thought of calling Gerald and telling him it was too late to send flowers, but she had suddenly remembered her and Shawn's letter to California, which she had forgotten to mail, and she decided to phone Margaret Lowe or Lang instead.

The long-distance operator tried to be helpful, but apparently there was a plethora of Longs and Lowes and Langs in Carmel, California. No Margarets among them.

"How about nursing homes?" Kate asked.

There was a "personal care" facility and Kate decided to try that. When the woman who answered understood that Kate was calling from clear across the country in Georgia and that she had a death message, she was impressed enough to pitch in and help.

"We only have one Margaret here," she said, "and her last name is Rittenbaum. Have you thought of trying the Alzheimer's home down the coast?"

Kate had Bets's letter before her, but the street address was so smudged she couldn't make it out.

"Do you have that number? I'll try it."

She wrote the number down, but then she hesitated to dial it. Suppose Bets's sister was mentally ill? If Bob Dunn considered her situation serious enough that he wouldn't notify her of her own sister's death, it was presumptuous of Kate to tell her—maybe even dangerous. And yet Bets had said she was going to her sister.

She decided to get somebody in authority—the superintendent or matron—and put it up to them.

The superintendent was a man. At first he was suspicious of Kate's query.

"I'm trying to get in touch with the sister of my neighbor, Mrs. Dunn," she began, floundering a bit in the face of his cold composure. "My neighbor died and her sister has not yet been notified."

"And the name?"

"Margaret . . . Margaret Lowe . . . Lang . . . Long. I'm not sure . . ."

"Oh, Margaret Lang!" said the man, laughing. "Miss Lang is the president of our board. She has an office here. I remember now that she has relatives in the South. Just a moment."

Now that she had communication practically within her grasp, Kate suddenly didn't know how to handle it. How do you say, *Your sister has been dead for a week—and how are you? Your sister has been murdered. Just wanted you to know.*

It was even worse that the low, cheerful voice that came on the line in California began with: "Bets? Hey, Sis!"

The man should have told her, given her warning, Kate thought.

She began by clearing her throat. "Miss Lang . . . Margaret . . . I'm Kate Mulcay, Bets's neighbor. Live across the road in—"

"Oh, in that darling log cabin!" caroled Margaret Lang. "I've seen it! How are you, and how is my sister?"

Kate swallowed hard. "I can't . . . I don't know how to tell you . . ." She faltered.

"Something's wrong with Bets? Go ahead. Tell me. I've been waiting for her and I've got to know."

"Dead," mumbled Kate. "Last week."

"Dead?" the woman whispered. "Bets is dead?"

"I'm sorry," Kate murmured.

"How? What happened? She wasn't sick! She was coming out here to stay with me! What happened?"

Kate told her about the blow to the head, the body in the fountain, Bob's decision not to tell her sister, and then his departure.

"The son-of-a-bitch killed her," the sister said fiercely. "I know it. She wanted to get away from him! I'm coming there to face him. Give me your number!"

Kate went to work, leaving Edge and Bambi lolling in deck chairs drinking coffee. She had forgotten to tell Bets's sister about the $100 and Shawn's larceny. She had promised to meet her at the airport as soon as Margaret could get an airline reservation and call her.

Meanwhile, there was a lunchtime meeting she had to cancel in order to get two columns written and be available to meet Margaret Lang's plane. Once a year, old political friends, some of them still in the legislature, which she had covered for years, and some of whom had moved on to other public jobs, met for lunch at Manuel's Tavern. The meal was usually a hamburger and a beer, but Kate loved the table talk. Half was reminiscence, half political gossip. Who would be named chief justice of the Supreme Court when the current justice's resignation went into effect? Who was going to run for Congress now that Representative Roy Rowland had announced his retirement? And sometimes it was earthier—which member of the powerful Appropriations Committee was divorcing his wife to marry a glamorous little law clerk?

Kate knew the half dozen men who gathered around

the lunch table and she could gauge pretty accurately how much was truth and how much wishful thinking by the politically ambitious. She liked the remember-whens and the boisterous humor and she hated having to cancel her part in this once-a-year gathering.

But as Shell pointed out, murder might out, but it wouldn't wait, and he now wanted a story on the two unsolved deaths in her end of the county. By the time she finished, it was six P.M. and Margaret Lang had called from the airport.

"I had to run to catch my plane," she explained, "so I didn't have time to call you. If need be I could get a taxi or one of your superior MARTA trains. I see them leaving the airport every few minutes. Should I grab one?"

"No, I'm coming to get you. Stand out front by Delta baggage. I'll be there in fifteen minutes."

Kate recognized Margaret right away because she looked so much like Bets except slimmer and perhaps a few years older. She wore a smart gray summer suit with a silk blouse and her hair was shorn into a short silver cap. She looked very tired.

Recognizing one another, they didn't bother with introductions. Margaret threw a small carryall onto the backseat and climbed in beside Kate.

"This is very good of you. I'm not sure I could have made the trip to Shining Waters without you—train, bus, taxi. I'm that tired!"

"You know, I'm relieved that you are here," Kate said. "I feel terrible about Bets and I wish I'd gone on and called you when it happened, in spite of what Bob said."

"He said, 'Poor thing, she's in a mental institution,' didn't he?"

Kate smiled at her. "Something like that."

"Well, how did you find me?"

Kate wished she'd thought to tell her before she asked because the purloined $100 in the dirty envelope was still inside her pocketbook. Without answering, she took it out and handed it to Margaret.

Margaret looked at the smudged address in her sister's handwriting for a few minutes before she opened it and saw the $100 bill. "Oh, Betsy," she said. "Little Betsy, sending me money to pay express on some of her stuff she had on the way. Boxes came, but I didn't hear from her."

They stopped in Roswell for a deli sandwich and a beer and Kate explained that she would ask Margaret to spend the night with her except for the presence of so many "blood kins."

"That's all right," Margaret said. "I have a key to Bets's house. You know . . ." she paused and bit her lips as if she might cry, "I guess that house belongs to me now. When I was here about a year ago, Bets and I made our wills, leaving everything to one another. Or could that have changed?"

Kate shook her head. "I don't know. Bets told me she was putting the house on the market and getting a divorce. I don't know how far she got with either project."

Margaret sighed and looked out the window. "At least it will be all right for me to spend the night in it, don't you think?"

Kate thought it would, but she wouldn't want to be the one to go alone into that dark and lonely mansion, not knowing where Bob Dunn might be.

Surprisingly, the Greens were in the Dunns' yard when

Kate delivered Margaret to the door. They had been swimming in the pool.

Edge had the grace to look a little embarrassed. Bambi looked defiant. Shawn looked glad to see Kate and drew as near to her as he could in his dripping bathing suit.

"The creek's more fun, Cuz'n Kate," he whispered as if apologizing for disloyalty.

Kate made the introductions and Margaret seemed indifferent to the Greens' use of her sister's property. She greeted them courteously and walked straight to the dark front door.

"Can I bring your bag in for you?" asked Edge, eager to redeem himself in the eyes of the Dunns' kin.

"Thank you," said Margaret, fumbling with the front-door key. "And then see if you can make this thing work."

Edge was eager to be of service and he did manage to get the door open and carefully place Margaret's carryall inside. He looked fat and hairy in his wet bathing suit and childishly pleased with himself, Kate thought.

Bambi, wearing wooden clogs on her feet and a towel around her plump midsection, had stalked off toward the cabin. Shawn hovered around Kate.

"I'll ride with you," he offered as she went to her car. "I got to tell you Miss Willie wants to take some plants to the cemetery for Theron's grave tomorrow. She said would you like to go?"

"I would," said Kate. "I'll drive. It's too far to walk with a load of plants."

Miss Willie was in Kate's backyard early with a trowel and a damp paper bag filled with red and white verbena, petunias, and lamb's ears. She had a dry burlap bag at her feet that was fragrant of cow manure. Kate saw her before she had drunk her first cup of coffee and she went to meet her, with a second cup for the old lady.

"Well, you don't aim to go in your josie?" Miss Willie said, looking disapprovingly at Kate's bare feet and frayed housecoat.

"No, ma'am," said Kate meekly. "You just caught me unawares. I'll put on some clothes when we finish this coffee."

Little Bright Prospect Church, one of the oldest left in the county, stood on a windswept hill with its graveyard spread out around it like an apron. The early morning sun painted the long bubbly glass windows set in the peeling white clapboard walls with a fiery light, but magnolias and mimosas shaded the old gravestones and the mossy paths, making a place of coolness.

Kate stood a moment looking at the sagging steps and the old double doors, spaced well apart to make separate entrances for the men and women. What hope, what valor to name it "Bright Prospect."

They found Theron's grave by the harsh red clay earth that had been piled up in the digging of it. Kate's florist flowers with the ugly purple bow were centered on the mound. There was a little painted vase at the head holding a crumpled bouquet of shattery crape myrtle.

"Arnie's, I bet," Kate said, touching it gently.

Miss Willie nodded. "The onliest pretty thing she had, I reckon."

Miss Willie knelt beside the grave, digging holes to ring it with flowers, and Kate hauled water in a bucket she found by the well to pour on them.

They sat for a moment on the church house steps when they finished, to admire their work.

"I wish Arnie would tell me what she knows about Theron's death—Bets's, too," Kate said.

"Let it be, child, let it be," Miss Willie said, standing up.

"I can't," Kate said, grinning. "You know I got to know."

"Did you know that that woman Charlene is kin to Arnie?" Miss Willie put the question idly, without apparent interest.

"How kin?" Kate asked quickly, wondering how close the relation was.

Miss Willie was walking ahead toward the car. "I ain't sure. There was a woods colt in it sommers."

"Miss Willie!" Kate said in mock exasperation. "Why, this thing was complicated enough and here you go putting an illegitimate baby in it! Who was the woods colt?"

"Say it was Arnie," Miss Willie said matter-of-factly. "That may be why she didn't inherit none of that Renty land yonder."

"Oh, for goodness' sake!" cried Kate. "That's absolutely benighted. Why, in England they make kings of their bastards."

"Now, Kate," said Miss Willie reprovingly, "you don't have to use bad language."

Kate smiled and started the car. "Just a technical term, Miss Willie," she said. "Not pretty like 'woods colt,' but not obscene, if that's what you mean."

Miss Willie was silent on the drive back to her house. Semantics were beyond her, but she knew what she knew. *Bastard* was a bad word and she didn't like it besmirching the lips of her friend Kate.

Kate was more concerned with what this information could mean to the current population of the county, but couldn't see the relevance just yet. She let Miss Willie off at her house without further comment and went home to bathe and dress for work.

Margaret Lang was standing by the back steps talking to Edge. She turned to greet Kate. Her face was pale without makeup, her eyes dark-circled.

"Did you get any rest last night?" Kate asked.

She shook her head. "Not much. I kept missing my sister. Where do you suppose that bastard Bob Dunn is?"

Page Miss Willie, Kate thought. *The word is with us again.*

Aloud she said, "I haven't a clue, but his lawyer was a close friend, I think, and you might talk to him. They were together the night Bets died. Let me get his number for you. He lives in the subdivision, I believe, and has an office in Roswell."

While she riffled through the phone book, she wondered what she could offer Margaret for breakfast. She returned to the steps with Addison Coate's office address and telephone number on a piece of paper.

"How about breakfast?" she said.

Margaret shook her head. "Not hungry, but I was wondering if you could spare Mr. Green to drive for me a couple of days? Bets's car is in their garage and the keys are on a rack by the kitchen door. I need to talk to the medical examiner and get a lawyer of my own. And I'm not familiar with the area. Besides"—she grinned—"I'm tired."

"Oh, I know Edge will be glad to drive for you!" Kate said.

He was beaming and Bambi had hurried to change from her nightgown to pants and a jersey. Margaret had not mentioned taking on Bambi, but she made no objection, and Kate was glad to see them following Margaret back to the subdivision. Shawn had disappeared in the direction of Miss Willie's creek with the two Gandy sisters.

Sweet peace, Kate thought, heading upstairs for a leisurely bath. But peace was short-lived. She heard a car in the drive and, wrapping a towel around herself, she parted the bathroom curtains and peered out.

Police.

I'm not budging, she thought. *Let 'em wait.* She turned the water on full force and for good measure threw in some of Bambi's bath salts.

Sergeant Corky Corcoran wasn't in any hurry. He sat on the back steps, turning a flashlight this way and that in his hands. When Kate joined him, feeling fresh and tidy in her best pale green linen, he offered no cheerful good mornings or how's-every-little-thing-Kate, a greeting left over from a childhood devotion to Fibber McGee and Molly on the radio. He looked glum and said darkly, "Where'd you get that bend in your bumper?"

"Bend in my bumper?" repeated Kate, thinking it sounded like a country song title. "I didn't know I had one."

She walked toward her car. Corky followed.

There was a sizable dent in her bumper. It was the newest car she'd had in years and she thought she was taking care of it on the theory that she might never have another one. Here was her bumper almost crushed against the radiator.

She looked at Corky in puzzlement.

"I don't know," she said. "I can't imagine when it happened."

"How about down at the borry pit three nights ago?"

"Corky Corcoran, you're out of your mind! Do you think I knocked that car in the borrow pit and ran over that boy? I can't believe it!"

"Beau's gon' ask me if you have a alibi. You got any witnesses that you were somewhere else?"

She started to say the Greens knew she was in the backyard until she heard the ambulance siren. She was talking to Shawn about the movie he had seen. But suddenly she was damned if she would call on them. Then she remembered the ambulance attendants and the small crowd of neighbors who were at the pit when she drove up.

"They know I came up after it was all over," she told him.

He smiled pityingly. "Kate, there's such a thing as hitting and running and coming back."

"That's right," Kate admitted, thinking about it. It was an old trick among criminals, especially unidentified hit-and-runners. She had covered more than one case where the culprit had with apparent innocence returned to the scene and taken the victim to the hospital. One grateful old gentleman was baffled by the resemblance of his benefactor's car to the one that hit him. He hated to say anything, but a nosy reporter—not Kate—had seen blood on the fender.

"Corky," Kate asked thoughtfully, "was there blood on my car?"

"We gon' check it out at the station," Corky said uncomfortably.

"You want me to drive it in? You can follow me and make sure I don't go by the car wash."

"Aw, Kate," Corky protested, but he agreed.

It seemed hours before Kate got her car back. A young policeman put it in the newspaper's parking lot and came in to tell her about it and enjoy a tour of the newsroom. He had planned to be a newspaper reporter, he said admiringly.

Kate understood. She had planned to be a policeman. They went by the snack shop for a cup of coffee and, although she suspected he wouldn't tell her, she asked if they had found any incriminating stains on her car.

He shook his head. "I didn't ask and they didn't say. Just took me off school-crossing duty to make the delivery. Otherwise you'd have had to pick it up yourself."

Kate thought he was telling her to be grateful for door-to-door service, but she only felt abused and wrongly suspected. Only when she walked the young officer to the elevator did it occur to her that her car might have been dented while Edge was driving it. *I hope to God he didn't hit anybody,* she said to herself. He certainly had not hit Theron, but if there was blood on her car, anybody's blood, it would justify Beau's tendency to treat her as a suspect.

The note on the kitchen door at the cabin said Margaret had ordered Chinese for all of them. Come on over. Kate slipped off her shoes and stepped into the battered loafers she kept by the kitchen door. She hung her jacket on the back of a kitchen chair and took the woods path to the Dunns' house, where she found Bambi presiding prettily over a table full of paper plates and plastic knives and forks on the screened porch.

Margaret, in shorts and sneakers, reclined on the wicker chaise, looking very tired. The damp heat plastered her hair to her skull and her sleeveless cotton shirt to her body.

She looked miserable, but she rallied a little at Kate's arrival and, smiling faintly, waved her to a wicker rocker.

"How did it go today?" Kate asked, sitting and accepting a beer from Edge, who seemed to be on duty.

"I learned a lot," Margaret said. "I saw Bob's lawyer, who was unctuous and awful and kept assuring me that the world mourned for my lovely sister. He had heard nothing at all about a divorce. From what he knew, Bob and Bets had a model marriage. No, he didn't know where Bob had gone. Isn't that the most ridiculous thing you ever heard? Of course he knows!"

"Did he know how Bob was going to get by without notifying you of your sister's death?"

"I didn't ask him. I forgot in the middle of his mushy hand-squeezing. But the next lawyer, Bets's, said he could have delayed telling me by one trick or another for time enough to collect her estate and get out of town. That is, as long as he wasn't implicated in her death. And I guess he wasn't."

"Did Addison know Bets had a lawyer?"

"Claimed he didn't. I went to the courthouse. Edge found it for me."

Edge, munching a fortune cookie, smiled proudly at the achievement. Any filling station attendant in the county could have directed them to the courthouse, but from where Edge sat it was a major accomplishment.

"Of course, I knew Bets had a lawyer," Margaret went on. "She shouldn't have married that jerk, but you know, she really loved him. She was several years older than he was and I guess he was handsome and sexy!"

"Um-um!" put in Bambi, giggling. "He is that!"

"He never made a dime and I think he persuaded Bets to come to the South so he could get his hands on our grandfather's money without my eagle eye watching him. She came. He spent and ran around and it finally got to be too much for her."

"So you found the lawyer's name at the courthouse?"

"Yes, on the divorce petition. She's a very smart woman. Black, graduate of Harvard, and so nice. She had a copy of Bets's will, which she is filing for probate. She also had a copy of the contract Bets signed with a real estate agent to sell the house. So it looks like . . ." she stirred restively on the chaise, "it looks like all the practical details are in hand. Now I want to know who killed my sister."

Kate pushed the plate half filled with lo mein back on the table. Suddenly she wasn't hungry.

"I want to know, too," Kate said soberly, standing up. "I think I have an idea."

Kate prepared to go, but apparently the Greens weren't ready and she had to find out about the dent in her bumper. She asked Edge to walk outside with her.

"The police are very interested in the dent in my car," she said. "They want to know how and when it happened. Do you know?"

"Gosh, Cuz'n Kate!" said Edge uneasily. "I meant to tell you about that. It was a pure-tee accident. Bambi didn't mean no harm. She was waiting for me in the car to go somewhere the other day and I took longer than she thought I should, so she started up and . . ."

"And hit something," Kate finished.

"That ash tree at the edge of the yard. It's kind of in the way anyhow. You have to maneuver to get around it."

"It hasn't been in my way all these years," Kate said dryly.

"Well, don't worry about your bumper," Edge said miserably. "I'm gon' get it fixed. I meant to do that before you saw it."

Kate shrugged and walked away. How could Edge get a bumper replaced? It was a childish hope and nothing would come of it. He couldn't afford it and the way things were going, she soon wouldn't be able to.

The next morning, instead of dressing for work, Kate put on her heaviest winter-wear jeans and boots and a long-sleeved shirt. She was going to walk through the woods to Arnie's shack because she wanted to get there quietly without attracting the little woman's attention. Like Mr. Renty, Arnie might run, and for some unaccountable reason, some odd intuition, Kate felt that she was the key to the killings.

She would have liked to have had Miss Willie along for company and to answer a few questions that troubled her, but she didn't want to be slowed up. Her ancient friend walked well, but climbing over rocks and up riverbanks was hard on her knotted old legs. She decided to avoid the path to the subdivision and Miss Willie's trail beyond and cut through Mr. Banana Pierce's old house site.

The sun had not appeared yet on the ridge beyond the pine thicket to clear away the tattered mist that hung over the river. Kate could wish for a cool day for Margaret Lang, who was accustomed to the northern California climate and seemed to be suffering from Georgia's heat as much as the sordid business of her sister's death. *Just wait,* Kate promised her silently, climbing a barbed-wire fence and trying to pick up the trail to the spring. *We never have the same kind of weather more than three days at a time here in the blessed foothills of the Appalachian mountains. Be patient.* But she was thinking of more than weather. If her hunch was right, Margaret Lang would be helped through the agonizing uncertainty of Bets's death. It would not bring her back. But there would be some kind of peace in knowing.

When she reached the river, Kate took off her sneakers and tied the strings together and hung them around her neck. She found a stout stick to use in determining the depth in the part of the river closest to the bridge and Arnie's house, with which she was not familiar. She rolled up her jeans, and considered taking them off momentarily until she remembered the fisherman in front of Arnie's shack.

She started wading. The little stream was icy, spring-fed, but it sang a pretty song, skipping over and around the big rocks, rushing over little falls, swirling to the bank and back again. Kate wished for Kim Sue and Sheena and Shawn and a better day when their presence would be for fun.

Presently she saw the rusty tin roof of Arnie's shack, and in the misty morning light it had a certain beauty. She waded close to the shore, peering into the alders to see if Arnie or any other fisherman might be there.

She clambered up the bank and, calling out to Arnie

and Clarence, she sat on the steps with her back to the closed door and started putting on her sneakers. The door creaked open and Clarence appeared, looking as if he'd slept in his rumpled jeans and jersey, with his long hair hanging in his eyes, which were swollen and bloodshot.

"Miss Kate," he said by way of greeting.

"Hi, Clarence," Kate said buoyantly. "How are you this morning? I want to talk to you and Miss Arnie."

"Miss Arnie ain't here," Clarence said evasively. "And I got to be going to my job. I'm a-working Theron's old job up at the Texaco."

"Where is Arnie?"

Clarence shrugged and shook his head, but his eyes wandered up the hill back of the house.

On impulse, Kate said, "Did she go up to the old Renty house?"

"I don't know."

Kate stood up on the rickety step and faced the gaunt, sad-faced scantling of a boy. "Clarence, you do know where she went and I think you'd better tell me all about it. Arnie is kin to Mr. Renty and Charlene, and somebody has gypped her out of her share of the property up there that must be worth almost a million dollars by now. Was it Charlene?"

"Miss Arnie don't care about that," Clarence said, shuffling his feet in their ragged running shoes and staring off across the river. "Miss Arnie wouldn't ask nobody for nothing."

Kate sighed. "I know that, Clarence, but now that her son is gone . . ."

"Well, I reckon she'll see 'em about that. Ain't nobody gon' git by with hurting Theron if she can hep it."

A sudden spurt of urgent energy took hold of Kate. She got to her feet and started running. At the edge of the yard she turned back.

"Clarence, did she take a gun with her?"

"Yes'm," the boy said.

"Oh, my God!" Kate cried. "Come on, Clarence, come on!"

Clarence came, not as fast as Kate wanted him to, and mumbling a protest with every step.

All she heard was, "Miss Arnie wouldn't want us. Hit's her bidness."

"I don't care!" cried Kate. "We got to stop her."

They caught up with Arnie at the edge of the Renty yard. The stuffed animals were back out along the picket fence, but they looked soggy, as if they had been there for days and had wilted under the mist that hung over the old house and yard. Only the bear with the fiddle in his hand was dry, sheltered by the tumbledown roof.

"Arnie," said Kate softly, touching the woman's thin shoulder as she walked toward the gate that still hung ajar. "Give me your gun."

"No'm," said Arnie, ducking her head and clutching a rusty old shotgun with both hands.

Kate turned to Clarence. "Run on ahead," she said. "Go to the back door. Warn Charlene. We can't let Arnie do this. Tell Charlene to get the hell out—as fast as she can!"

She put an arm around Arnie. "Come on, honey," she said. "Let's rest a minute. I'm tired and I know you are."

The face Arnie turned toward her was numb and expressionless. Her dark eyes were the eyes of a wounded animal, staring blankly.

Clarence came around the corner of the house. "I don't see nobody," he said. "I called and nobody answered."

Kate sighed with relief and steered Arnie to the steps. She wanted to start her back to the shack on the river, but even if Arnie was willing, Kate doubted that the thin little woman had the strength for the walk. She sat down on the edge of the porch and pulled Arnie down beside her. Arnie clung to the shotgun, resting it between her knees.

"You got a lot against Charlene, I know," Kate began soothingly. "Her side of the family . . ."

"Yes'm," Arnie said, staring off into the distance. After a moment she said humbly, "I was a woods colt. My grandpa throwed my mama out, afore I was born."

"And left his property to Charlene's folks?"

"No'm." A wisp of a smile crossed the wrinkled little face and was gone. "They didn't git nothing, neither. Uncle Eli got hit all."

"Then why . . ." began Kate, puzzled.

"Charlene kilt my boy. She tried to kill Uncle Eli. She kilt that woman down yonder that was married to the man that's a-laying with her. He wants this land." She tilted her head to indicate the fields and acres that surrounded the house. "And I reckon she wants to live in that there fancy house nigh you."

"You right," said a voice behind them.

Kate turned quickly. Charlene stood in the doorway with a heavy oak pole in her hand. The battling stick, Kate thought, the one that beat Mr. Renty, the one that killed Bets. A plain old lye-stained stick that was once used to beat the dirt out of work clothes on wash day.

"Charlene . . ." Kate began, "put down your stick. I'm

gon' take Arnie home and we can work this all out some other time."

"Yeah," jeered Charlene, "with the po-lice. I know you. You'll spill your guts to them buddies of your'n."

There was movement in the hallway behind her. Bob Dunn in his underpants, weaving drunkenly. The sun, just beginning to rise, caught his jowly, unshaven face, his glazed eyes, his bare hairless chest ornamented with a big lipsticked red heart.

"Go on back, lover," Charlene said over her shoulder. "Git in the bed. I'll be there t-reckly."

Her half turn to speak to him gave Arnie the opportunity she wanted. She raised the shotgun and fired.

Bob Dunn fell. Charlene, screaming wildly, knelt beside him. Kate crawled over the porch to where he lay. The blast apparently left him alive, but both his legs were a bleeding mess, torn off at the thigh.

She dimly heard the shotgun hit the magnolia tree at the edge of the yard. Clarence had wrested it from Arnie's hands, thrown it out of reach, and picked her up, and was running toward the road with her.

It was the last Kate saw before a blow on her head knocked her unconscious.

When Kate came to, she was on her feet, but she couldn't move them or her arms. She thought it must be night because she couldn't see anything and her head ached horribly. She tried to move her body and presently realized that it was immobilized by a wall of some kind. A coffin? she wondered. But they didn't stand coffins on end and she was upright.

The pain washed over her in waves, making her alternately nauseated and sleepy. She didn't know how long she had been there when she heard voices.

Miss Willie and the children. And another voice . . . she wasn't sure whose. Her mind drifted off into a fog.

Some time later, she didn't know how long, the voices were closer and she tried to move and cry out, but she couldn't.

"Hit's blood," Miss Willie was saying. "A heap of blood. Kate . . . I wonder where she coulda went to."

Kate tried to speak, but there seemed to be a gag in her mouth. She tried to move, but the walls imprisoning her were too tight.

She heard Shawn say something about a bear, and one of the girls—Sheena?—said, "Mr. Renty, make him play us a tune."

Hands were moving near her and Kate suddenly realized where she was. Inside Charlene's bear!

Somewhere near her aching head something moved and the thundering timpani and shrill fiddle music of "Dixie!" battered against her ears. The pain was excruciating.

Oh, let me move, let me move! she prayed silently.

With superhuman effort she made her body lurch against the bear's stomach wall.

"Look, he moved!" cried one of the girls.

"The bear's dancing!" cried the boy voice of Shawn.

Kate made another effort to move. And then she fainted.

When she came to, she was lying on the porch and Miss Willie was bathing her face with cold water.

"Miss Willie knew bears can't dance," Shawn was saying proudly. "She knew where to look for Cuz'n Kate."

"They can, too, dance, bears can," said Kim Sue, launching an argument that was interrupted only by Mr. Renty passing around muscadines he had found ripening in the woods.

Miss Willie sent the girls to the paved road to ask a passing motorist to call the police and an ambulance. The old woman was mortified days later when Kate reminded her that there had been a telephone somewhere in the Renty house.

Kate chafed at her confinement in the hospital, mainly because she was humiliated that an unathletic woman like Charlene had been able to knock her out with the battling stick, roll her into the hide of the bear, and push her and the bear to an upright position. This before she apparently loaded an unconscious Bob Dunn into her car and got him to the hospital.

"And I thought carrying Mr. Renty down the hill was pretty major," she said jealously.

She had been home only a few hours, enjoying a late-day drink in the backyard swing, when Clarence came walking down the road.

Arnie had hanged herself!

He had found her body swinging from the oak tree in the yard when he got home from the Texaco.

"Oh, the poor thing!" cried Kate. "The poor little thing!"

"Yes'm," said Clarence. "But without Theron . . . And then the po-lice would be atter her, wouldn't they?"

"I don't know." Kate sighed. "I would say she was justified . . . or mentally unbalanced . . . or maybe both. Oh, poor little Arnie! She probably could have moved to the old Renty homestead now. Charlene's in jail and Bob Dunn will be when they can get him out of the hospital."

"Yes'm," agreed Clarence. "But Miss Arnie didn't want nothing nobody else had."

Kate moved the swing slightly and lifted her eyes to the trees above her. *The moon is confounded, the sun ashamed,* she thought, borrowing a line from the book of Isaiah. What will become of Clarence now?

Margaret Lang came to say good-bye. She was not as surprised as Kate had been that Bob had been having an affair with a coarse and uneducated woman like Charlene. He had met her when some fellow clock collector told him she had an exceptionally fine timepiece.

"Oh, he liked refinement, all right," she said. "I think he even coveted it, having been raised poor himself. But he coveted money more and a thousand acres of land up here made that gaudy little broad look enticing. Especially when he was drunk." Her eyes sought the subdivision across the road. "At least he won't get Bets's house. It's still on the market. Until it sells . . . I wonder what you would think of my employing Mr. and Mrs. Green to live in it and take care of it? They could have the use of Bets's car, of course."

Kate's bruises and the knot on her head still hurt too much for her to get up and grab hands and spin into a dance with Mr. Renty, who came capering across the yard with a yellow bowl on his head and a dirty Braves tie flapping across his chest.

Instead she smiled and said politely, "I think that's a wonderful solution."